THE LADY COURTS A MARQUESS

Ladies of Seduction
Book Two

Jillian Eaton

© Copyright 2025 by Jillian Eaton
Text by Jillian Eaton
Cover by Dar Albert

Dragonblade Publishing, Inc. is an imprint of Kathryn Le Veque Novels, Inc.
P.O. Box 23
Moreno Valley, CA 92556
ceo@dragonbladepublishing.com

Produced in the United States of America

First Edition February 2025
Trade Paperback Edition

Reproduction of any kind except where it pertains to short quotes in relation to advertising or promotion is strictly prohibited.

All Rights Reserved.

The characters and events portrayed in this book are fictitious. Any similarity to real persons, living or dead, is purely coincidental and not intended by the author.

ARE YOU SIGNED UP FOR DRAGONBLADE'S BLOG?

You'll get the latest news and information on exclusive giveaways, exclusive excerpts, coming releases, sales, free books, cover reveals and more.

Check out our complete list of authors, too!

No spam, no junk. That's a promise!

Sign Up Here

www.dragonbladepublishing.com

Dearest Reader;

Thank you for your support of a small press. At Dragonblade Publishing, we strive to bring you the highest quality Historical Romance from some of the best authors in the business. Without your support, there is no 'us', so we sincerely hope you adore these stories and find some new favorite authors along the way.

Happy Reading!

CEO, Dragonblade Publishing

Additional Dragonblade books by Author Jillian Eaton

Ladies of Seduction Series
The Duchess Takes a Lover (Book 1)
The Lady Courts a Marquess (Book 2)

Prologue

Lily & Grove Dress Shop, London, England

It was a known fact that whenever Lady Harmsworth had a titillating piece of gossip to divulge, she had a tendency to flush. And that morning, as she marched through the front doors of Lily & Grove Dress Shop, her entire face was the approximate shade of an overripe tomato.

"You are *never* going to believe what I just learned!" she exclaimed, her bosom bouncing as she threw her arms into the air with great dramatic flair.

"If you've come to tell us about the Duke and Duchess of Southwick, we've already heard," said Lady Farthing, muffling a yawn. "Their reconciliation is already old news."

"I think it's wonderful." This from Lady Topple, the only spinster in the trio. Despite already being five and twenty, she still clung to the hope that her future husband was out there, somewhere. And he had a great affinity for cats. "True love won out in the end, as it is meant to."

"Maybe for *them*," said Lady Harmsworth, arching a heavily plucked brow. "But what about the Earl and Countess of Radcliffe?"

Lady Farthing visibly perked as she stepped off the dais where she was being fitted for a new gown and shooed the seamstress away with a curt flick of her wrist. "Oh? What about them?"

"Do you mean the Duchess of Southwick's sister?" asked Lady Topple, frowning.

It was public knowledge that, despite their meager social beginnings, Marabelle and Katherine Holden had gone on to make *excellent* matches when they'd married the Duke of Southwick and the Earl of Radcliffe, respectively. While rumors of turmoil had recently followed Marabelle, Katherine had thus far escaped all whispers of marital strife. Not an easy thing to do in the *ton* where affairs were more plentiful than Lady Topple's cats.

Of course, there was the little matter of the tragedy that had occurred right *before* Lord and Lady Radcliffe were married... but no one talked about that. At least no one with any sense of self-preservation, for who would dare incur Lord Radcliffe's wrath?

The earl was, in a word, terrifying.

Even speaking about him now, in the seclusion of the dress shop, made the fine hairs on Lady Topple's nape stand on edge.

"Yes," said Lady Harmsworth, nodding. "That's precisely who I mean. I just heard from Lady Greene, who heard from Lady Henley, who heard from Lady Button—"

"Get on with it," Lady Farthing snapped. As the mother of six unruly children, she'd lost her patience years ago. Occasionally it could be found in the bottom of a wine bottle, but she made a point of never drinking before noon. Except on Mondays. And Wednesdays. And some Saturdays. But this happened to be Tuesday, and that meant she had another three hours of sobriety to endure.

Lady Harmsworth pursed her lips. "Well, suffice it to say, I have it on excellent, firsthand authority—"

"Firsthand?" Lady Farthing said incredulously. "You just prattled off half the members of the Grosvenor Square Historical Society!"

"Agatha! Do you want to hear about the divorce or not?"

"Lord and Lady Radcliffe are petitioning for a *divorce?*" Lady Topple gasped. "No. They can't be."

"Oh, but they can." Lady Harmsworth couldn't have looked more like the cat that had got the cream if she'd suddenly sprouted whiskers. "And according to Lady Greene, per Lady Henley, per Lady Buttonwood—"

"Shoot me now," Lady Farthing groaned.

"—that is *exactly* what the Countess of Radcliffe intends to do."

Lady Topple sank into the nearest chair and shook her head in disbelief. "I can hardly believe it. An affair, perhaps. Even a separation like the Duke and Duchess of Southwick had. But a divorce? It's unheard of."

"Parliament will never allow it," said Lady Farthing.

"Lord Greer was granted a divorce last year, in addition to the right to remarry," Lady Harmsworth pointed out. "Besides, *I* certainly wouldn't want to be the one who tries to tell the Earl of Radcliffe what he can and cannot do. Especially after what he already did."

"You shouldn't speak of such things, Agatha!" said Lady Farthing.

Lady Topple nodded in mute agreement.

Lady Harmsworth rolled her eyes. "Why not? Everyone already *knows*. Just because it is not discussed openly doesn't mean it didn't happen. Personally, I don't blame poor Lady Radcliffe for trying to escape him before it happens to her."

"He wouldn't dare do it again," Lady Topple whispered, aghast. "Would he?"

"You know what they say," Lady Harmsworth said with a shrug. "Once a murderer, always a murderer. He killed one woman and got away with it. What's to stop him from killing another?"

CHAPTER ONE

April 1813
12 Hill Street
Mayfair District

"WHAT DO YOU mean, you won't go forward with the divorce?" Kitty demanded, driving her heel into the carpeted floor as she glared at her husband. He was sitting upright on his large, canopied bed, an open book on his lap and a full glass of brandy on the table beside him. In the muted candlelight, his features appeared even sharper and more forbidding than normal.

Handsome, yes—the Earl of Radcliffe was almost impossibly handsome. But there was a ruthless edge to all of that brooding beauty.

An edge she'd sliced herself open on more than once.

"It's late, Katherine," William sighed, and he knew—he *knew*—that she hated it when he called her that, which only served to spike her temper higher. "Can't we get some sleep and address this in the morning?"

She shouldn't have come in here. They kept separate chambers for a reason, and it wasn't due to goodwill. For while the Countess and Earl of Radcliffe presented a united front outside Hill House, their London manor, inside of it they'd taken to keeping as far apart as two people could be while still living under the same roof. But if the first glass of wine she'd imbibed in the parlor downstairs had bolstered her courage, then the second had spurred her into action. And since she'd already climbed the stairs . . .

"We can address it *now*," she seethed.

"There will be no divorce." He gave a casually, infuriatingly dismissive wave of his arm. "There. It's done."

A myriad of emotions swirled through Kitty's body at her husband's proclamation.

Fury.

Hopelessness.

Anguish.

"But you said—" she began before he cut her off with an impatient snarl.

"I was not being *serious*, Katherine. I spoke of divorce in a moment of anger. You know as well as I that it isn't a feasible option."

"It could be," she persisted stubbornly. "If we petitioned the courts—"

"No," he said flatly.

"But you don't *want* to be married to me!" The wine bubbled to the tip of her tongue, putting words there that sobriety kept at bay. "Not when you love her."

William closed the book he'd been pretending to read with a violent snap. "I said I don't care to speak of her."

"Why not?" Kitty said shrilly. "She's always right here, whether we speak of her or not. In our house. In our carriage. In our *bed*. She's here all the time, and I for one am sick of it. I won't live like this, William. I won't have three people in this marriage when I only said vows to one."

A thundercloud rolled across the Earl of Radcliffe's countenance. When it had cleared, he raised his hand in the air and crooked his finger. "Come here, Katherine."

"I don't want to," she said, shaking her head from side to side.

"Katherine—"

"*Fine.*" Her feet dragged over the floor as she obeyed his summons. His arms shot out and he caught her around the waist, swinging her easily up and onto his lap. At first, she wanted to deny him. To resist the traitorous feelings swirling around inside of her. Feelings of lust. Of longing. Of desire. But it was a futile endeavor.

Her mind may have hated William, but her body . . .

Her body was helpless to resist him.

And while they didn't have any of the other traits that made for a good marriage—love, trust, respect—they had *this*.

They'd always had this.

Sheer, unadulterated passion.

William's book fell to the floor with a soft *thump* as she straddled him, her ivory nightdress skimming to the top of her thighs while the blue wrapper she'd donned before daring to enter her husband's bedroom followed the direction of the book. He cupped her jaw on a low rasp of breath as she leaned toward him, her breasts, unbound by constraint or corset, rubbing against the rigid expanse of his chest.

"Kitty," he murmured, and she melted into his kiss, her lips parting to welcome the bold slide of his tongue while hers flicked into the cavern of his mouth where she tasted the warm oak of brandy and the barest hint of peppermint.

She slid her fingers through his hair, nails gliding along thick, silky, wheaten tendrils before anchoring at his nape when the kiss deepened and he yanked her closer to the hot, hard heat of his loins. Sparks, bright as fireworks exploding over Vauxhall Gardens, ignited in her belly as she rubbed herself along his throbbing length, a moan of frustration stealing from her lips at the rough, restrictive barrier of the trousers he preferred to wear to bed in place of a nightshirt. Her fingers left his hair to fumble at the row of brass buttons holding his manhood captive, but before she could unfasten the first one he lifted his hips, simultaneously dropping her onto the mattress whilst yanking his trousers off.

Naked, he pounced, his lean, muscular body enveloping hers in an iron embrace.

"We said we wouldn't do this again," he said harshly, his brown eyes burning black as he wavered between desire and restraint. A battle that Kitty had no intention of fighting.

"We lied," she purred, arching her spine off the bed to bring them together.

A flash of fire, a rumbling growl of assent, and the Earl of Radcliffe—renowned for his self-control—captured her mouth in a bruising kiss while one of his fingers parted the curls below her navel to slide seamlessly inside her velvet sheath.

She clenched around him, her wet muscles contracting, and carried his groan of approval deep into the base of her throat. Bowing his head, he took her nipple into his mouth and sucked in tandem with the glide of his hand, establishing a rhythm of ebb and flow that had her writhing shamelessly atop the linen coverlet.

The wall sconces on either side of the bed began to sputter as on top of the mattress, Kitty and William's desire soared to new heights. She panted his name and then cried it when his fingers drove her over the edge, but before her nerve endings could find a soft landing amidst the heady thrum of pleasure he flipped her over onto her side and entered her from behind, his hand biting into the curve of her hip as he buried his staff to the hilt in a thrust that robbed them both of their breath in the very best way.

She closed her eyes and saw flashes of light, bursts of color that exploded across an ebony swath of starless night. This was how it had always been when she was wrapped in William's arms. It was when she was *out* of them that the trouble began. But there was no room to think about that here, in this sacred place, in this sacred moment, when their bodies were entwined and their skin was slick with perspiration and passion.

"*Katherine*," he rasped into her ear and this time the sound of her full name didn't annoy as much as it enthralled. He pushed her hair to the side and kissed the side of her neck, the soft, intimate gesture making her toes curl even as the rest of her demanded more.

He thrust again and her entire back bowed, lust humming through her veins. Bracing an arm above her head, she flattened her palm against the engraved mahogany headrest as he withdrew and then drove forward, carrying her right up to the brink . . . and then over it on a sharp cry of release.

She might have said his name. She wasn't sure. She wasn't sure of anything as her vision blurred and warmth flowed through her body in a soft, dewy unraveling; the first blush of sunlight after a long, cold night.

He sought his own satisfaction immediately after, his breath hot and harsh against her nape while his abdomen contracted and he pulled her tight against him, merging them together until it was impossible to tell where he ended and she began. And for the tick of a minute, for the length of a miniscule eternity, they clung to each other. To what had been their past, however brief. To what would never be in the future. He stroked her hair, gently combing out the tangles. She closed her eyes and ran her fingers along the arm he had draped over her side, allowing her defenses to weaken and waver in the afterglow of a desire that refused to be denied.

She didn't *want* to want William.

Not like this.

Not with an insatiable hunger that she felt in her bones.

In her very *being*.

It would be easier, so much easier, if their physical appetites had waned along with their tolerance for each other. But it was as if the harder she tried to untangle herself from him, from their empty husk of a marriage, the stronger the bonds of their lust became.

And it was tempting—oh, so tempting—to settle for this. To let these stolen nights, fueled by fury and frustration, be enough. To let their passion be enough. But she wasn't going to be her mother. She wasn't going to *settle* for crumbs when she deserved the entire bloody pie. If William couldn't give her all of himself, then she would take none of him. Tonight was just another mistake. Another lapse in judgement. As was the night two days ago . . . and the afternoon a week before that.

Seven months' worth of mistakes.

But her *biggest* mistake was ever agreeing to marry William in the first place.

Stiffening, she began to withdraw from his embrace, and after a token display of resistance he lifted his arm, watching with a shuttered, unreadable gaze while she gathered her belongings.

"You're going to your room," he said.

"Yes." She held her nightdress to breasts that still throbbed from his kisses. "I want a divorce, William."

A muscle ticked in his jaw. "You can want it all you like. My answer remains the same."

Anger and the vestiges of desire quickly cooling brought twin splashes of pink color to her cheeks. "But we're miserable together! Why not separate and find happiness individually?"

"It's out of the question."

"William—"

"*Go!*" His thunderous roar made her eyes widen. William's emotions ran deep, and he rarely let them rise to the surface. But when he did . . . when he did, the heavens rumbled. "If you cannot abide my bed, if you cannot abide *me*, then go, Katherine. Seek your own room. Seek your own company. But you'll do it under the Goddamned roof that we *both* share. As husband and *fucking* wife. Is that understood?"

Glaring, she drove her heel into the floor and quit the room without another word.

CHAPTER TWO

Five Days Later
12 Hill Street
Mayfair District

K ITTY WOKE IN a mood.
This, in and of itself, was not remarkable.
Blessed (or cursed, depending on the day) with a volatile temper, Kitty often found herself mired in *some* sort of a mood. Unlike her older sister, Mara, who held her emotions at arm's length, Kitty wore what she was feeling on the edge of her sleeve. She always had, even when she tried not to. Even when she bit her tongue so hard it bled.

A consequence, she supposed, of being raised in a household where contrary opinions—or opinions of any sort, really—weren't only not permitted, they were punished. While black and blue bruises had bloomed on top of Mara's skin when she took the blows meant for both of them, guilt had festered under Kitty's. It had twisted and tangled into long, stringy weeds until she had an entire garden's worth of shame running through her veins.

It was that shame, that secret hidden garden of atrocities, which had initially propelled her toward William. Toward an earl that Society said she couldn't have. Toward a husband that her heart had wanted in spite of the shrill warnings from her head. And wasn't that fitting, wasn't that just bloody *wonderful*, because now William was the one man she wanted to escape.

Unfortunately, it still wasn't going very well.

Thus explaining the mood.

"What do you mean, he's not here? Where is he, then?" she growled at Stevens, William's personal valet and gatekeeper. He was short and stout, with a bald head and a series of lines across his temple that had a tendency to deepen with disapproval whenever she entered his line of sight.

Ever since Kitty had become the Countess of Radcliffe, she and Stevens had found themselves at odds. Before then, really, as he'd closed the door in her face not once, not twice, but *three* times. The self-important little toad. He couldn't lock her out of the house any longer, but he did take glib delight in refusing to divulge his employer's whereabouts. And to Kitty, for whom outward appearance was everything, having a servant openly defy her was ... well, it was infuriating. Almost as infuriating as being ignored by her husband.

"I am sorry, my lady." Stevens squared his shoulders and stared at a spot on the wall directly behind her right ear. "Lord Radcliffe has yet to return from his previous outing. I could not say with certainty where he is at the moment and would not care to speculate in regard to his whereabouts."

Kitty gritted her teeth. "But we had a meeting planned for noon, and it's already half past one."

"It's not like Lord Radcliffe to be tardy." Stevens brown gaze met hers for an instant, then swept away with a dismissive flick that made her grind her teeth even harder. "I am afraid you're likely mistaken on the time. Come to think of it, I do not recall any such meeting in his daily schedule of events. Perhaps it's for tomorrow?"

"We both know it's not for tomorrow, Stevens." She glared at him, daring him—*willing* him—to commit a truly dismissibleworthy offense, but as per usual the valet was well aware of right where the line was... and how to keep his webbed toes on the correct side of it. "When you see my husband, kindly remind him that my time is just as valuable as his, and I don't like to have it wasted."

"Of course, my lady," Stevens smiled.

She smiled back. "Thank you."

They both turned away, knowing that Stevens would never do anything of the sort. And after donning her pelisse and bonnet, Kitty stepped outside into the warm spring air, inhaling the sweet, floral scents of lilacs and daffodils.

It was a marvelous English spring. Clear blue skies, chirping birds, blooming wisteria. Everywhere she looked, people were smiling and children were laughing. Even the stray dogs were wagging their tails. Why, then, did she feel like a bucket of lead was lodged in the middle of her chest, so heavy that when she walked, the heels of her shoes dragged along the ground?

Adjusting the wide brim of her straw poke bonnet so that she wouldn't have to make eye contact with random passersby, Kitty adopted a brisk pace that further discouraged conversation and directed her steps toward Bond Street. If there was anything guaranteed to raise her spirits, it was shopping. Specifically, shopping with her husband's coin. If she couldn't get William's attention one way, then by God, she'd try another... and buy herself a few presents in the process.

By the third store, she was feeling marginally better.

By the fifth, she had begun to smile.

By the seventh, she was positively beaming.

"Put the diamond necklace on Lord Radcliffe's account," she said airily, turning in a circle inside the glittering confines of Longfellow's Jewelry Emporium, "and the matching bracelet on my wrist. I prefer to wear it out."

"Yes, my lady." The owner, Mr. Longfellow, a shrewd businessman who had recognized a woman in need of spending a small fortune the instant Kitty walked into the store, snapped his fingers. "You heard the countess, she'd like to wear the bracelet out. Remove it from the case at once, and have the necklace wrapped for delivery." He paused. "Lady Radcliffe, before you depart, I would be remiss if I did not show you our most exclusive item. It came yesterday, and has not even been put out on display yet."

"Oh?" Kitty asked, a golden brow rising as she held out her wrist to one of the shop assistants. "What is it?"

"A brooch," said Mr. Longfellow in a hushed voice. "Rumored to have been worn by Lady Isabel Laurent and gifted to her by none other than the Duke of Sommerville during his marriage to Princess Antoinette of Luxembourg. It's a priceless piece. An heirloom, really. But her descendants have fallen on hard times, I'm afraid, and—"

"Everything has a price when you're pushed hard enough," Kitty interrupted. Ignoring the twinge in the center of her chest courtesy of the wire wrapped around her heart that had been tightening, tightening, *tightening* ever since her wedding night, she gave an imperious lift of her chin. "Show it to me."

Mr. Longfellow disappeared behind a velvet curtain for several minutes. When he returned, he was carrying a small black box. Setting it on the glass counter, he removed the lid with reverence to reveal a red ruby brooch surrounded by diamonds. "If I may be so bold, Lady Radcliffe, the coloring would look exquisite paired with your complexion."

The brooch was beautiful. Stunning, even. A truly remarkable piece.

But as Kitty, who naturally coveted all things pretty, stared at the brooch, she didn't feel impressed or in awe. Instead, she felt slightly nauseous. Because while the brooch *was* lovely, the story of how it had come to be was not. Princess Antoinette had given her husband fifteen—*fifteen*—children. And this was how he had her toil and allegiance repaid? By giving a priceless gemstone to his mistress?

Maybe if she didn't know what it was like to be chosen second by the one man in all the world who should have chosen her first, it wouldn't have mattered. But she *did* know and it *did* matter. It mattered very much.

"I am not interested," she said, turning her head away.

"But my lady—"

"Did I stutter, Mr. Longfellow, or otherwise make myself unclear?" Her voice cracked across the shop like a whip, freezing everyone in their tracks and revealing that despite her diminutive stature, Kitty was capable of exuding great force. If her sister's anger was a woeful gale, then hers was a wild tempest, howling and raging as it crashed upon the shore, destroying everything in its path.

When she was a child, her temper had been impossible to control and had earned her more slaps and bruises than she cared to remember. As she'd gotten older, she had learned the benefit of harnessing its power, of portraying herself as a sweet, agreeable woman until it no longer served her best interest. Because if there was one thing she would never do again, it was make herself weak or vulnerable to anyone.

Not to a shopkeeper.

Not to her husband.

Not even to her dead father, the monster whose vicious hands had sent her running into the arms of a suitor incapable of loving her . . . so long as he loved another. But she'd married William anyway, for what choice did she have when *she* loved *him*? It was a mistake that had caused her more misery over the past seven months than all the years she'd endured living under her father's fist combined.

Black and blue marks faded with time, but heartache?

Kitty's mouth twisted in a bitter smile.

Heartache endured when nothing else did.

"Have my purchases wrapped and delivered by end of day," she said coolly. "I'm sure you know the address."

Sunlight shimmered off her new bracelet as she departed the shop. Stopping to allow a flower seller with a wooden cart overflowing with tulips to pass by, she turned blindly to the left with no specific destination in mind, the brooch—and the thoughts it had invoked—having soured her desire for baubles and bonnets.

She'd find another way to gain William's notice.

Maybe she'd buy an elephant and move it into his study.

Or maybe she'd threaten to take a lover, as her sister had done.

Except William *liked* animals (he kept an entire pack of hounds at their country estate in addition to a stable filled with fine thoroughbreds), and she doubted he'd care if she became another man's mistress so long as she was discreet about it. What had worked to fix her sister's marriage was not going to work to fix her own. Because there was nothing *left* to fix. Nothing but hurt, resentment, and anger.

It hadn't started off that way, Kitty reflected as she sought temporary respite on a bench in the shade of a flowering cherry, its branches heavy with pink blooms. Tragedies didn't begin with heartbreak. No, for a relationship to be truly tragic, it had to start with hope. With happiness. With the alluring promise of true love. A good tragedy made you fly before it let you fall. And my, how had she flown. High enough to touch the clouds and beyond, to the stars.

Their story had begun as most did: with a look across a crowded ballroom. A look that had lasted less than a second. A look that had promised her heaven... before sending her plunging straight into hell.

CHAPTER THREE

May 1811
Haversham Ball
London, England

KITTY WORE BLUE to the ball. The fetching color complemented the rosy blush of her cheeks and her yellow silken curls piled artfully around a tiara adorned with diamonds. Only she knew that the gown was an old one of her mother's, the diamonds were made of glass, and that she'd purposefully worn elbow-length gloves to cover the light spattering of bruises that encircled her wrist like a ghastly purple bracelet.

Her entire appearance was an illusion. An illusion designed to fool her peers into believing she was something that she wasn't. She was an actress. The Haversham Ball was her stage. And she was about to put on the performance of a lifetime.

She heard the whispers as she glided past her peers, holding a long-stemmed glass of champagne as if she hadn't a care in the world.

"I thought it would be her," they said.
"The poor dear must be so embarrassed."
"At least she can be supported in spinsterhood by her sister."
Kitty's top lip curled at the last, a dog preparing to bite, but

she managed to school her expression into a pleasant smile before her fangs showed.

Spinsterhood?

She was barely twenty!

And older siblings were *meant* to marry before the younger. But when that older sibling was engaged to marry the Duke of Southwick, it cast a long shadow . . . a shadow that was impossible to fill given this Season's worm-riddled crop of bachelors. And the worst of it was that they were right. It should have been her getting married first! It should have been her marrying a duke. She was the fashionable one. The sociable one. The one that had gotten her and Mara invitations to the bloody Glendale Ball in the first place! But instead of noticing *her*, Southwick had set his sights on Mara. Sweet, quiet, bookish Mara who hadn't even been looking for a husband.

Now Mara was almost a duchess, and Kitty was already being labeled as a spinster! The unfairness of it made her stomach hurt. But she wasn't about to resolve herself to the fate that the *ton* had already decided for her.

Absolutely not.

She hadn't come this far to give up, and she damned well hadn't come this far to settle for being known as the sister of a duchess.

Tilting her head back, Kitty drained the contents of her champagne flute in a single swallow. The bubbles prickled on her tongue before sliding pleasantly down her throat and into her belly, warming her from the inside out. Removing a silk fan from her beaded reticule (another piece of her patched together wardrobe inherited from her mother), she flicked it open and used the scalloped edge to disguise the direction of her stare as she studied the men in attendance.

The Duke and future Duchess of Southwick weren't amidst the guests spinning around Lord and Lady Haversham's ballroom. Her sister had bowed out this morning, citing a megrim, and left Kitty scrambling to find a suitable chaperone as their father was certainly not an option (even if he hadn't already been passed out drunk on the parlor sofa by the time she was ready to leave). She'd landed on Lady Staffordshire, the mother of a friend, and had navigated an escape from the older woman's line of sight shortly after their arrival, leaving her to peruse her options for marriage at her leisure.

The good thing was that she hadn't many requirements. Aside from being titled and wealthy, they had to be under the age of forty and in possession of the majority of their teeth. Hardly a long or exclusive list. But as her gaze swept around the room, Kitty was pressed to find just *one* gentleman that met her prerequisites.

There was Lord Danver, a marquess, but he was closer to fifty than he was to forty and had already been married three times.

Lord Waverly would have been an option if she hadn't recently learned of his debts.

Mr. Brimes didn't have a title.

Sir Ridgley wasn't titled enough.

It was like being stuck in the middle of the desert searching for a glass of water . . . but all the cups were filled with sand.

Annoyed, she began to lower her fan . . . and then she saw *him*.

The man who would steal her heart and ruin her life.

But of course she didn't know that yet.

He was tall, so tall that she wondered why she hadn't seen him immediately. A black coat, exquisitely tailored, conformed to broad shoulders and muscular arms. A white cravat, run through with a gold pin, was wrapped around a strong neck kissed with a hint of bronze. His jaw was clean shaven. His nose long and straight. Blond hair, cut evenly at the nape, was combed back from a square temple. His entire countenance was a combination of hard, perfect angles. And his eyes . . . Kitty's stomach sucked inward as she drew a sharp breath. His eyes were a dark, piercing sable. The color of soil after a soaking rain or coffee before cream was added.

Those eyes watched her with the intensity of a hawk circling above a rabbit as he drew closer, the crowd parting out of his way without a word needing to be spoken. When he stopped in front of her and bowed, she gave a coy flutter of her fan and performed a curtsy, sweeping her blue skirts expertly to the side and affording him a teasing glimpse of her ankle if he cared to steal a peek.

He did.

Impossibly, his gaze grew even darker.

"Lord William Colborne, Earl of Radcliffe, at your service, my lady." His voice was rust over iron and the sound of it, both rough and refined, sent a shiver of awareness racing through her.

"Lady Katherine Holden," she purred, offering her gloved hand.

He took it, his fingers curling under hers for a second longer than necessary before he raised her arm and pressed his mouth to her knuckles. "A pleasure," he murmured, and if Kitty were the swooning type, she might have wilted then and there. But while everything about her was intended to imply she was a gently bred lady who would tremble and quake at the sight of a spider, Kitty was more likely to grind up the arachnid under her heel than run away from it.

"I can assure you the pleasure is mine." Her head canted. "How is it we've not yet met, Lord Radcliffe? I've attended every ball this Season, and this is the first time I've seen you."

"I was traveling abroad until recently. A business venture with a partner in Boston."

"And what, pray tell, was the manner of your business?"

He was still holding her hand, a fact that they were both very cognizant of even as they committed to pretending that they weren't. Below the soft rise of her palm, the rapid throb of Kitty's pulse gave away what her cool expression did not: she was wildly, madly attracted to William Colborne. In a way she'd never felt before, despite her brief dalliances with a few rogues who had been quite inventive with their tongues but not quite marriage material.

Was it possible that she'd finally found someone who was both? A suitor who made her thighs tremble *and* one who was titled? She'd have preferred a duke, but in desperate times, surely an earl would suffice. Kitty wet her lips. Could this be it? Could he be what she'd been waiting for, *whom* she'd been waiting for?

What would it be like, to not live in fear?

What would it be like, to not have to cover bruises?

What would it be like, to be certain of her next meal?

She wanted to find out.

How *desperately* she wanted to find out if this was the man who was going to save her from the pit of pain and despair she'd been trying to claw her way out of ever since she was a young girl. A young girl hiding under the bed with Mara's hand covering her mouth while their father stomped down the hall, bellowing her name.

"Dance with me," her knight said, those fierce, hawkish eyes burning into hers. There was a touch of gold in the mahogany that she hadn't noticed when he was on the other side of the ballroom. Up close, with his face mere inches from her own, it was like a streak of firelight across a black canopy of night. "Dance with me, and I'll tell you."

"Are you bargaining with me, Lord Radcliffe?" she asked, her lips curving.

"Indeed," he said simply, and her smile widened as they kept their hands clasped together and seamlessly joined the other couples on the floor already in the midst of a contra-dance . . . the very same dance she'd enviously watched her sister engage in with the Duke of Southwick less than a month ago.

The complicated steps required her to change partners, but even as she was spun away from William, she did not lose track of him in the sea of pastels, nor he of her. Thrice their gazes met, and on the fourth he gave a subtle jerk of his chin in the direction of doors that opened onto a sprawling stone terrace. It was not so much an invitation to join him outside where shadows blurred the lines of propriety as it was a command, and the quickening of Kitty's breath had little to do with the demanding movements of the contra-dance as she discreetly extracted herself in order to follow the earl out of the ballroom.

But when she slipped unnoticed onto the terrace, taking care to close the doors behind her, William wasn't there. A warm spring breeze stirred the damp curls at the nape of her neck and cooled her flushed cheeks as she turned in a circle, bemusement creasing her brow. A wide staircase, illuminated by torches set in raised marble basins, led to a garden with towering hedgerows and climbing roses.

Had he gone down to await her amidst the thorns?

Was he lurking in the midnight, a marble statue come to life?

Trepidation licked on the heels of nervous excitement as she took a step forward... and was abruptly yanked back when a pair of strong arms encircled her waist, dragging her into the darkness of a covered alcove.

"Don't scream," Lord Radcliffe murmured, his chin hovering above her shoulder. "It's only me."

It's only me, said Lucifer as he crooked his finger. *Don't be afraid.*

Desire gathered inside of her, a bowstring being drawn taut. She spun around in his embrace, her fingertips finding purchase on the diamond cut lapels of his tailcoat. The fabric was heavy and rich to the touch—a reminder of what *real* wealth felt like. Gazing up at him through a thick veil of golden lashes, she deliberately traced the tip of her tongue along the plump swell of her bottom lip and watched, delighted, as a muscle ticked high in his jaw.

"Who are you?" he said hoarsely, and she knew he hadn't forgotten her name. This was a deeper question. A question she wasn't sure she had the answer to. Who *was* Lady Katherine Holden?

She was the daughter of a monster.

She was the sister of an angel.
She was an actress.
She was a flirt.
She was a reckoning.
"Kiss me," she whispered. "Kiss me, and I'll tell you."

A true gentleman would have had the decency to deny her request, or at the very least put on a show of hesitation. But if there was one thing that was clear in the enigmatic swirl of fog that surrounded them, it was that William wasn't a gentleman . . . and she wasn't a lady.

Not tonight.

Not with *him*, the devil in a black tailcoat.

He cursed before he kissed her, an oath of absolution before condemning them both to the fiery clutches of sin.

Kitty held fast to his jacket as the sheer force of their combined lust knocked her onto her heels. William grabbed her by the hips, his large hands spanning across her bottom as his tongue plunged between her lips to taste and to take all that she had to give. He devoured her like he was a man half-starved and she offered herself up as if she were a feast, her fingers streaking up along the rigid plane of his chest until they reached the corded muscle of his neck, nails biting into his skin through her gloves.

Angling his head, he deepened the kiss even further, taking them to depths that she hadn't even realized existed despite her previous encounters with passion.

Puddles, she thought dimly. She'd been wading in puddles and now she was swimming in an ocean so vast there was no end of it in sight. And that was good, that was wonderful, because she didn't want it to end. Had she no need for sunlight or sustenance, she would have stayed here forever, wrapped in shadows and William's sensual embrace.

The broad hands cupped around her backside tightened, pulling her up against the pulsing length of his arousal. Shockingly hot, it seared her belly like a brand. Begging—*throbbing*—for the attention that a staff of its magnitude so rightly deserved.

The earl groaned against her lips when she groped him there, not with the grasp of a shy virgin (which she still, surprisingly, remained, at least in the practical sense of the word), but the sturdy grip of a woman who understood the benefits of receiving pleasure . . . as well as giving it.

She stroked with the same rhythm that he'd used to kiss her, a consuming tempo that guided her wrist from root to tip where a bead of seed had already caused a damp circle to form in the crotch of his impeccably fitted trousers. The physical manifestation of his desire encouraged her boldness and quickened the tempo of her hand as he wrenched free of her mouth with a low, harsh growl that was more animal than human.

Releasing his right hand from her derrière, he reached between her thighs, ruthlessly seeking and finding the source of her own lasciviousness atop the layers of muslin and silk taffeta that comprised her gown.

Beyond shame, she leaned into the hard edge of his palm, grinding herself on him. From somewhere inside the ballroom, laughter ensued, its shrill sound piercing the hazy cloud of passion that had enveloped them. Blinking, Kitty began to raise her head until William captured her mouth in another searing kiss and the laughter was forgotten . . . until the doors swung outward and they broke apart with dual curses. Through the velvet veil of obsidian, their gazes met and held.

Hers, heavy lidded and smoky with desire.

His, sharp as the edge of a blade.

"Lady Katherine."

"Lord Radcliffe," she said coyly as a group of men spilled out onto the terrace to light cigars.

"Excellent weather we're having."

"Quite."

A glint of humor shone in the rich brown of his irises. "I should like to call upon you tomorrow morning if you're available."

"I'll have to check my appointments," she said even as her

heart threatened to skip a beat. "I am a very busy person."

"Not too busy for an excursion around Hyde Park, I hope."

Circles of orange flared as the decadent scent of tobacco filled the air.

"I shall see what I can do, my lord."

He moved closer. Closer than he should have now that they had an audience. "Be ready at half past ten."

She looked past him while at her sides, her fingers curled inward, nails biting into her palms in a concentrated effort to prevent herself from leaping into his arms and demanding that he finish what he'd started. "That sounds more like an order than an invitation."

"Interpret it as you'd prefer." His words tickled the shell of her ear. "But be ready, and wear blue. It suits you."

Arrogant bully, she thought silently.

But what did that make her if she liked it?

"I'll be ready when I want to be, and I'll wear what I wish," she said with a rebellious toss of her head.

"Blue," he repeated. "It matches your eyes."

Those blue eyes flashed. "You can't tell me—"

But he was already gone, melting into the darkness as if he were made of it.

CHAPTER FOUR

April 1813
A bench on Bond Street
London, England

A FROWN SHAPED Kitty's lips as she forcibly withdrew herself from her memories. Despite her best attempts to keep them at bay, they always had a way of sneaking up on her. Not unlike the tiny, feathering creases in the corners of her eyes that she slathered with cream every morning and every night. Cream that stank of tallow, but what did it matter what it smelled like so long as it worked? A woman in a world ruled by men had precious few things that genuinely belonged to her, and her beauty was paramount amongst them.

If she was granted a divorce from William—*when* she was granted a divorce from William—she would need to rely on her appearance to ensnare another husband. A wealthy husband. A malleable husband. Most importantly . . . a husband she didn't love. Because she couldn't go through this again. She *wouldn't* go through this again. One divorce was going to be scandalous enough. It would set the entire *ton* on its heels. The gossip mongers would have fodder for months, if not years. But she'd rather live on whispers than suffocate in a marriage where another woman was taking up all of the oxygen.

Kitty glanced at her new bracelet as she rose from the bench. William disapproved of her expensive tastes, which made her new purchase all the more satisfying. She pictured his countenance when he received the billing note from Longfellow's. The grooves that would bracket the edges of his already stern mouth. The shadow of ire in his steely gaze. The tick of disapproval in his jaw.

She should have bought two.

Idly plucking a cherry blossom, she twirled it between her fingers as she set off toward Mayfair by way of Winslow Park, a small sanctuary of green tucked away amidst the busy streets and businesses. Birds flitted in and out of the winding shrubbery, tufts of stolen horsehair and other treasures held in their beaks as they built their nests. A rabbit sprang out of the underbrush, startled at the sight of Kitty, and then dashed away with a bounce of its white tail. Ducks circled in a small pond, their paddling feet creating small ripples in their wake as they glided effortlessly across the water's glossy surface. It was a beautiful view to behold. A calming view. And for a moment, Kitty stopped walking and allowed herself to drink it all in.

Too often, it felt like she was running in a mad race with no discernible finish line.

Running away from her childhood.

Running to keep up with her peers.

Running toward a secure future.

Running to escape her husband.

When would it all just *stop?* When she and William were first married, she'd thought . . . but no. If there was one luxury she did not permit herself, it was the luxury of daydreaming about lost hopes and ruined expectations. What was the point? What was broken could not be *un*broken. Not so long as her heart belonged to William and his heart belonged to another.

Scowling at a sparrow as it flew across the compacted dirt path, she continued onward. Distracted by her own thoughts, she failed to notice when someone fell in step behind her. Not until they gave her a hard shove while simultaneously yanking her bracelet hard enough to break the tiny clasp.

"*Stop!*" she cried as soon as she'd regained her balance and realized what had happened. "Stop, you thief!"

The pickpocket, a young lad by the look of him, delivered a mocking grin over his shoulder before he skipped off down the trail, the bracelet clutched triumphantly in his fist. Any other lady would have likely resigned herself to the loss, which was undoubtedly what the pickpocket counted on when lifting items of worth from this section of London—hysterical, swooning women who cried into silk handkerchiefs as they watched their material possessions being carried away. But Kitty wasn't any other lady.

And no one took what belonged to her.

"You little shite," she snarled as she unbuttoned her pelisse and cast it aside. "That's *mine*." Necessity had taught her to be fast as a child—a father couldn't hit what he couldn't catch—and she'd retained that athletic nature into adulthood. Without the tight confines of long sleeves, her arms swung freely as she took off after the pickpocket, her legs moving as fast as her skirts would allow.

They rounded a bend and he peered back again, his grin falling away and his eyes widening under the brim of a misshapen brown hat when he saw that Kitty was in hot pursuit. He sped up and so did she, anger fueling her steps. Anger caused by far more than a nicked bracelet.

"Oi!" he shouted in protest when she grabbed him by the collar. "Git off me, ye maniac"

Kitty grunted in pain when a pointy elbow jabbed her in the ribcage. Releasing his coat, she pinched his ear, giving it a hard twist that earned her a stomp on her instep. They both cursed as they fell to the ground in a flurry of punches and kicks, rolling around on the grass like a pair of street cats hissing and clawing.

The boy wasn't overly large—he couldn't have been older

than ten or eleven—but he was surprisingly strong, and tears sprang to her eyes when he pulled her coiffure. In return, she sank her teeth into his forearm, biting straight through his patched coat to the skin underneath.

Howling, he relinquished his hold on her hair and drove his knee into her stomach, causing all of the air to leave her lungs in a loud *whoosh*. Sputtering, she managed to latch onto his ankle as he tried to crawl away, heaving her upper body over his leg so that he couldn't drive his boot heel into her chin.

"Return my bracelet and I'll let you go," she gritted. The pickpocket tried to turn over, but she held fast, using her superior weight to her advantage. "I said *return it!*"

"All right then! Bloody 'ell!" He tossed the bracelet and Kitty dove after it, staining the tips of her gloves when she scraped her fingers through the grass. Securing the diamonds, she clambered to her feet and whirled around just as the thief was preparing to scamper away.

"Halt!" she ordered. "Halt, or this will be the last piece of jewelry you ever steal. The Bow Street Runner I send after you will make sure of that. It's hard to take things that don't belong to you when you're in prison."

With a groan, the thief froze in place, his shoulders dropping dejectedly. "Ye got yer piece back, didn't ye?" he grumbled. "What else do ye want?"

"An apology, to start with." Through narrowed eyes, she took a closer look at her adversary. He was whip thin and nearly as tall as she, with bony shoulders that stuck out of a threadbare jacket and trousers that stopped a few inches shy of his ankles. Her gaze traveled up the length of his arms to where his hands hovered in midair. His petite, suspiciously delicate hands. "Turn around. Let me see your face."

With obvious reluctance, the thief obeyed her command.

"Lift your head."

"Why the 'ell—"

"Should you like me to trounce you again?" she challenged,

taking a half step forward.

The boy jerked his head up, revealing a pale, freckled face smudged with dirt beneath a tangled nest of brown hair. But it was what was *under* the dirt and the snarled curls that gave Kitty pause.

High cheekbones. Arching brows. Long lashes framing belligerent green eyes.

"You're a *girl*," she blurted, nearly dropping the bracelet in her surprise.

"The 'ell I am," the pickpocket retorted.

"How old are you?"

"Dunno." A bony shoulder jerked. "Ten, maybe. I don't keep track."

"Ten?" Almost a young woman. Susceptible to all the world's evils. Evils that Kitty understood better than most. "Where do you live?"

"What do ye mean?"

"Where is your *home*, girl?"

"Ain't got one of those. And I told ye—I'm not a girl. I'm a boy."

"Yes," she said impatiently, "and I'm the Queen of England. Do you have any parents?"

The pickpocket shook her head.

"Siblings? A cousin, perhaps?"

"Don't have anyone."

Kitty took great pride in her ability to hold herself at arm's length from everyone around her, including her own sister. Including her own *husband*. No one could hurt her or disappoint her if she remained aloof and unfeeling. If she kept what remained of her heart under lock and key. Aside from Mara and William, she had no family to speak of, not since her father had died. She had no close friends, no cheery servants to lend an ear and impart wisdom. She was on an island that she'd made for herself, and that was just the way she liked it. The way she *wanted* it.

The defiant glint in her pickpocket's eye was uncomfortably familiar.

"Come with me," she snapped. "You need a warm meal and a hot bath. I'm sure you have lice crawling around under that mop of hair."

"I don't have any bugs." The freckles on the pickpocket's nose bunched together as her nose wrinkled. "And I'm not goin' anywhere with ye."

"Yes, you are. There is really no point in arguing." Kitty began walking. For a moment, there was only silence behind her, and she wondered if the girl had fled. Not that it would matter. She was in the midst of trying to leave her husband. The last thing she needed was a scrawny, lice-infested pet to care for. But then she heard the light pitter patter of footsteps . . . and a strange, unfamiliar warmth unfurled inside of her chest when the pickpocket trotted up beside her.

"What's your name?" she asked, keeping her gaze on the path in front of them. "I need something to call you other than *thief*."

"What's *yer* name?"

"Lady Katherine Colborne, Countess of Radcliffe." She paused. "You can call me Kitty."

"Everybody calls me Jack." The pickpocket kicked a stone. It bounced across the dirt before rolling into the grass. "But me mum called me Jacqueline."

"Ah, yes, Jacqueline," said Kitty dryly. "The archetypal boy's name."

The girl muttered something undecipherable under her breath as they exited the park and turned left onto freshly swept pavement. In the midst of Mayfair, the most prestigious district in all of London, grand rowhomes set back behind wrought iron gave way to even grander single homes, distinguished from their smaller counterparts by enormous marble pillars, peaked dormers, and second story balconies. Cherry trees lined the street, filling the air with a sweet, floral scent and the ground with a blanket of pale pink.

"What happened to your mother?" Kitty asked, flicking a bloom off the capped sleeve of her morning dress. Too late, she remembered that she'd taken off her pelisse and left it in the park. She'd have to send a servant for it, as they were nearly home. If someone made off with it in the meantime, well, better she lose a pelisse than a diamond bracelet.

"My mum died." Jack's green eyes went big as tea saucers underneath a choppy fringe of auburn as her head swiveled from side to side. "Bloody 'ell, is this where ye *live?*"

"Yes. Right here, actually." Kitty nodded at a rectangular metal placard engraved with the number twelve. Opening the gate, she ushered Jack inside, then motioned for her to stop before they'd gone halfway up the limestone footpath that led to the front portico. Beyond the portico was a brick manor covered in white stucco with green ivy creeping up the side. Square in shape and comprised of four stories, the manor was notable for both its sheer size and the symmetry of its architecture. "Before I allow you in, I've a few rules you must abide by."

"Rules." Jack turned and spat into the bushes. "Ye didn't say anything about no rules."

"Rule number one"—Kitty held up a finger—"no spitting. Rule number two, no stealing. Rule number three, no cursing."

"Bloody 'ell. What else is there to do?"

"I don't suppose you know how to embroider."

"I stabbed a boy with a needle once when he tried to grab my tit." Jack smiled at the memory. "Squealed like a stuck pig, he did."

"Rule number four, no stabbing." *This*, Kitty thought silently as she escorted her feral charge into her house filled with beautiful, breakable things, *might be a worse idea than marrying William Colborne.*

>>>><<<<

WILLIAM WAS IN his study, head bent over a ledger tallying the business expenses from his most recent investment, when the door opened and Kitty waltzed in unannounced.

He'd heard her when she had arrived home, of course. His wife was many things. *Quiet* wasn't one of them. But her sudden appearance was unusual, as normally she did her best to avoid him during the day. Then again, ever since she'd sunk her claws into the notion of divorce, she had taken to hounding him whenever it pleased her to do so.

At first, he'd humored her. If it soothed her ruffled feathers to rant on about a legal separation, then he wasn't going to argue for the sake of arguing. They did enough of that already. He had assumed—wrongly, as it turned out—that the idea of divorce was merely a passing fancy. Like the time she'd suggested they move to Charleston, or when she'd briefly entertained the thought of becoming an actress. Kitty was a fountain of spontaneous ideas. But ever since she had returned from visiting her sister the month prior, the dissolution of their marriage had remained first and foremost on her mind.

"As you can see, I am quite busy," he said without looking up. Truth be told, he hadn't the energy for another fight like the one they'd had five nights ago when he'd let his temper get the better of him and spoken to her in a way that he now regretted. Being married to Kitty was like standing in the eye of a hurricane. There were entire hours, days, even weeks where the skies were clear and the sun was beaming. But then the winds would shift, the skies would darken, and the storm would whip through, clearing everything from its path.

Theirs had always been a volatile love.

Not violent—he'd never harm a strand of hair on that gorgeous, infuriatingly stubborn head.

But from their first kiss on the terrace to the cruel words they'd flung at each other like knives in the dark, he and Kitty had always teetered on the edge of passionate madness.

"This won't take long." She closed the door behind her, and William pinched the bridge of his nose until black dots danced behind his closed eyelids.

"I said that I was—" He stopped short when he opened his eyes and saw her. The heavy silk drapes framing the windows were partially closed (he concentrated best in low light), but the dim interior of his study did nothing to disguise his wife's disheveled appearance . . . or the thin line of red scratches on the side of her neck. "What the hell happened?" His chair flipped over as he shoved away from his desk. With fury darkening his countenance, he stalked to her and grasped her chin, turning her face from side to side to survey the damage done. In addition to the scratches on her neck, there was a dappled bruise slowly forming on her arm and a tear in her skirt. "Who the *fuck* hurt you, Katherine?"

"No one," she huffed. "Well, someone. I've brought them here."

"Where are they?" he snarled, red clouding the edges of his vision as he dropped her chin and spun toward the door. "I'll kill them."

"No, you won't, because they are here as a guest. *She* is here as a guest."

"She?" he repeated, his brows gathering. "You mean to say a woman did this?"

"A girl, really." Kitty fussed with the lace hem on her sleeve, then raised her gaze to his. "Her name is Jack, and she is going to be staying with us until she can find gainful employment or steals all of our silver, whichever happens first." At his hard inquiring stare, she sighed and went on. "It happens that Jack is a bit of a pickpocket and attempted to steal my diamond bracelet."

"You don't have a diamond bracelet."

"I do as of this morning." She smiled brightly at him. "After Jack and I had a . . . discussion . . . about whom the bracelet rightfully belonged to, I invited her here. She needs food and a bath. A series of baths, preferably, as I doubt one is going to scrape off all the layers of grime."

As the bloom of crimson faded from his visage and his roaring pulse resumed its regular rhythm, William stalked back to his desk, righted his chair, and sat down to glare at his wife across piles of neatly sorted parchment. "We are not harboring a common thief."

"I wouldn't say she's *common*." Kitty twirled a loose curl around her finger. "She reminds me of myself at that age, and I'd like to help her."

Help her? God help *him*. One Katherine was enough, but two? The house would be burned to the ground by the end of the week.

"No," he said flatly.

"You'll hardly know that she's here."

"Kitty—"

"I'll put her in the east wing of the house. As far from the silver as she can get. You'll hardly notice that she's here," she repeated. His wife's smile turned razor sharp. "Given that you hardly notice *I* am here, I doubt it will be a difficult accomplishment."

"*Kitty*—" But he was talking to empty space. She was gone.

William purposefully counted to three, and then picked up a small glass orb resting on the corner of his desk. A useless decoration intended to keep papers in place. Thoughtfully, he passed it from his left hand to his right, fingers curling reflexively around its smooth dome shape. When he threw it across the room, it struck a bookcase and exploded on impact, scattering shards of glass everywhere.

How easy it was to shatter something fragile. Breaking delicate things took hardly any effort at all. It was putting the pieces back together again that was difficult. Sometimes even impossible, as what was broken could never *really* be made whole. At least, not in the way it once was.

As he stared at the fragments of the glass orb, William found himself contemplating his marriage. Where it had started, where it had ended up, and where it had all gone wrong.

So fucking wrong.

CHAPTER FIVE

May 1811
32b Canary Street
London, England

WHEN WILLIAM WAS invited into the private residence of Eriam Holden, the first thing he noticed was the smell. Dank and damp, like flowers left in a vase to wilt. The second thing he noticed was Lady Katherine... and the color of her dress. Not blue, as he'd requested, but a creamy pink that brought out the shimmers of gold in the soft curls surrounding her heart-shaped countenance.

The defiant tilt of her chin as she performed a flawless curtsy in the doorway of the parlor told him that the choice had been a deliberate one, and the sardonic pull of his lips let her know that her challenge had been received.

"You look as lovely as a rose in bloom," he told her, and to his further amusement she merely nodded, as if the compliment was not only anticipated, but a due to be paid for the privilege of being in her presence.

Some might have deemed Katherine conceited, but William liked her confidence. A woman who was sure of herself was a beautiful creature indeed, and in his twenty-three years of life, he'd yet to witness Katherine's equal. When he'd spotted her last night across the ballroom . . . well, it would be poetic nonsense to say that the world had shifted on its axis. But *something* had moved, compelling him to approach her when it was in his nature to do the opposite. Even then, he'd expected his interest to quickly wane. But after their kiss on the terrace, she was all he had thought about. All he could *think* about. And the hours from then to now had crawled like a slow eternity of torture.

"What do you have planned for our outing, my lord?" Long lashes, a shade darker than her flaxen mane, swept down, concealing the brilliant blue of her irises as she continued to hover in the doorway.

"A carriage ride through Hyde Park, if you would still find that enjoyable."

"I find *all* sorts of riding enjoyable," she purred throatily.

William's stomach clenched. Leaving the platter of lukewarm coffee and crumbling biscuits that a maid had brought out upon his arrival untouched, he crossed the parlor and stopped directly in front of her. The air between them vibrated with tantalizing awareness, and were they back in the web of shadows that had shielded them from sight at the ball, he wouldn't have hesitated to yank her against him and plunder her mouth with his own. But there were rules when it came to young ladies (thus explaining his general avoidance), and even he wouldn't go so far as to compromise a woman in the middle of the morning whilst standing in her family home.

"Lady Katherine," he gritted.

Her lashes slowly lifted. "Yes, my lord?"

"Is your father available?" Behind his back, William's hands curled into fists as he struggled to restrain his baser instincts. A foreign battle, as he was typically a man of supreme composure. Nothing rattled his cool, calm sense of control. Nothing, it seemed, except for Katherine Holden. "I should like to speak with him before we depart."

The warmth faded from the room with the speed and completeness of a candle snuffer dropping over an open flame.

"My father is currently indisposed." Tension radiated along the elegant line of her jaw as she turned her head to the side. "Is your carriage outside? I've an appointment later in the afternoon that I cannot be late for."

"It is," he said, studying her closely.

William understood the complicated relationship that could exist between a parent and their child. He had one with his own father, a boisterous, careless wastrel who would have haphazardly destroyed seven generations of wealth had William not continuously intervened and dragged him from the gambling hells by the scruff of his collar.

As the second-born son, Henry Colborne had spent most of his life wallowing in self-indulgence after marrying a pretty debutante and producing a male heir—the bare minimum required of him. But when his brother—William's uncle—had snapped his neck racing phaetons in the park, Henry unexpectedly found himself crowned as the new Marquess of Kentwood.

Overwhelmed by the vastness of the fortune at his disposal, he'd spent a quarter of it within a year and had been well on his way to running through the rest before William, with the aid of his grandfather, the Duke of Cumberland, who had always been more of a paternal figure to William than his own father, managed to reel Henry in.

Since then, the marquess's health had taken a turn for the worse. All those years of drinking and sleeping with anything that moved had finally caught up with him, leaving Henry mostly bedridden with ailments that ran the gamut from gout to venereal distemper. A sad, but not undeserved ending for a man who had systematically squandered every opportunity handed to him, quite literally, on a silver platter.

"If we're to go out in public, then you should have a proper chaperone." Unable to stop himself from touching her, William glided his thumb along her cheekbone as he tucked a strand of hair behind her ear. "If your father is not available, is there no one else that can accompany you?"

"I have an older sister, but she is attending a dress fitting." A shadow flitted across Katherine's face, there and gone in a blink. "Mara is getting married at the end of the month. To the Duke of Southwick."

"Why aren't you with her?"

"Why do you ask so many questions?"

He didn't . . . usually.

But he could see sadness there, behind the self-assuredness and sharp quips that Katherine built around herself like a wall covered in thorny roses. Sadness that he wanted to rip out with his bare hands, even if it made him bleed. Another foreign sensation that he didn't know entirely what to do with. So he took a step back, to where the footing was more familiar.

"This was a mistake," he heard himself say, his tone painfully dry and formal. It was the tone he used when he spoke with his grandfather. A tone forged in the midst of a chaotic upbringing.

A child being raised by children.

Wasn't that what his governess had said when she thought he wasn't listening? When he'd been pretending to sleep upstairs while his parents had cavorted below in a drunken orgy of depravity and opium. Or, as they'd referred to it, another ordinary Tuesday evening. But perhaps he ought to be grateful, for it was the combination of all those Tuesday evenings that had made him who he was today, a man of remarkable discipline and self-restraint. A man who recognized the weight and worth of his title. A man who had no intention of following in the footsteps of a spendthrift scoundrel.

His behavior at the ball had been an exception, not the rule, he saw that now. He saw, too, that to be around a woman like Katherine was to illicit the sort of dangerous temptations that his father had fallen prey to. Temptations he'd done his damned best to avoid.

"I apologize for wasting your time, my lady. I'll see myself out." He bowed stiffly, then waited for her to step aside and let him pass.

Instead, she tilted her head and pursed her lips.

Lips capable of making even the most pious priest succumb to sin.

"If you are going to waste my time, Lord Radcliffe . . . then at least make it worth my while." Her heel jutted back, and the *click* of the latch plate as the door swung closed was as loud as a gunshot in the enclosed space.

Heat pooled in his loins and he was pike hard even before she grabbed his waistcoat and pulled herself up to his mouth. A tease of a pause, a hint of sanity, and then they were right back on that terrace, in the dark, where shadows blurred reality and caution was a thing to be thrown to the wind.

The door rattled on its hinges as he shoved her against it, one hand cushioning the middle of her back while the other tangled in her hair, sending pins flying in every direction. He swallowed her moan; it tasted of desire and desperation, the kind that threatened to consume a man whole even as it slyly beckoned him closer. Even as it bid him to abandon all rational thought in exchange for raw, unadulterated lust.

She nipped his lower lip and he growled before returning the favor, using his tongue to soothe the bite before plunging it between her lips to feast in a cavern of silky, sensual delights.

At the ball, he'd detected a hint of champagne dancing on her breath. This morning, it was peaches. Rich, ripe peaches. The sort that dribbled juice down your chin when you sank your teeth into them. And that's what he wanted to do to her. To kiss, lick, and nibble all the sweet parts of her body until his mouth was wet from her wanting.

Until it was *soaked*.

Her breasts overflowed into his palms when he adjusted his grip on the curves of her body, and she gasped when he flicked his thumbs across her nipples, the points already pressing boldly against the thin fabric of her bodice and the flimsy excuse for a corset she wore underneath. A simple tug and the dress would fall to her waist, exposing inch upon delicious inch of pearly skin to the dappled morning light streaming in through the windows.

As he pictured her clothed in sunshine and nothing else, it took whatever fleeting control still remained in his possession not to free his rock-hard cock, pin her hands above her head, and take what he *really* wanted. What every piece of him was humming for. What every part of his being wanted more than his next breath.

If he stopped now, it was just a kiss.

A kiss to trounce all kisses in the history of mankind, but still . . . just a kiss.

Nothing more.

If he stopped now.

Propriety warred with passion as he peeled himself off her and raked his fingers through his hair, grasping the strands by the roots. Requiring distance, he stalked to the nearest window and stared blindly through the clear glass, his mind a muddled mess.

Maybe he had more of his father in him than he cared to admit.

Or maybe his loss of control came courtesy of a half years' worth of celibacy, as he'd not slept with a woman since ending his affair with a comely widow over the winter. That wasn't to say he hadn't sought relief by his own hand, but there was a marked different between a man's own palm and the soft, yielding flesh of a woman.

Just as there was a difference between a widow and a debutante.

Scrubbing his hands across his face, William started to turn, a formal apology already poised on the tip of his tongue . . . only to find Kitty leaning lasciviously against the door, her spine arched in a way that put her ample bosom on full display and a hand splayed suggestively below her navel.

"Are you ready to go?" she asked, raising a brow. "Or should we stay here and resume our . . . activity?"

If they stayed, he'd have her bent over the sofa in a matter of seconds.

Suddenly, a ride through Hyde Park sans chaperone didn't seem so scandalous.

"After you, my lady," he said roughly, gesturing at the door, not trusting himself to take his hands off her if he touched her again.

"Thank you, my lord." She sauntered into the foyer, her lovely derriere attracting the full, unabashed weight of his gaze. A gaze that jerked hastily upright when she abruptly halted and peered at him over her shoulder. "Lord Radcliffe?"

"Yes?"

A dimple he'd not noticed before winked mischievously in her cheek as she tapped her nose with a gloved fingertip. "Eyes up here, if you would."

"My eyes are up, Lady Katherine." But as he followed her out the front door, William was left to wonder how the hell he was going to keep them there.

※

AFTER THEIR FIRST circle around one of Hyde Park's less-traveled bridlepaths, Kitty fancied herself smitten by Lord William Colborne. By the end of the second, she was convinced that she'd fallen in love. This was not a particularly unusual event; by her count, she'd been in love no fewer than two times before. But the severity of the fall . . . that *was* notable.

When she was a girl of fourteen with stars in her eyes, she'd tripped over Lord Theodore Plinkton but had quickly recovered her balance after she wrote out Lady Plinkton in her journal and found the name to be distasteful.

A year later, she'd kissed James O'Connor in the broom closet and had almost dropped to her knees (and not just because he'd asked her to). But once she'd recovered from the shine of his blue eyes, she'd realized that a stable boy, while undeniably handsome, could not provide her with the future that she sought.

Since then, she'd been more careful with her heart. What remained of it, anyway, after an upbringing that had hammered it down into a shape that was hardly recognizable. But as she sat across from William in his gleaming black barouche carriage pulled by a pair of quality gray thoroughbreds, Kitty found herself quite flat on the ground. And it wasn't *just* because he was wealthy, titled, and sinfully attractive (although those things certainly didn't hurt).

It was the way he held her when he kissed her. As if they were lost at sea in the midst of a storm and he was keeping her head above water.

It was the way he looked at her. As if she were a vice he didn't want but an addiction he couldn't quell.

It was the force and power he exuded. As if he were a man who was accustomed to getting every single thing that he desired, no questions asked.

But there *were* some downsides that she needed to consider. He was only an earl, not the duke that she'd had her mind set on. He also wasn't a husband who would be easily manipulated into doing whatever she wanted.

But what alternative did she have?

As soon as Mara was married, she would move out, and Kitty would be left to fend for herself. It was no secret that her sister had taken many a vicious blow caused by *her* impertinent tongue. Mara was the obedient daughter, Kitty the willful, and their father . . . their father was a monster whose drunken rages had led him to do terrible, terrible things.

Like murdering their mother.

But they didn't talk about that.

Kitty didn't even like to *think* about it.

Because some secrets were meant to be kept, and the night Eriam Holden had shoved his wife down the stairs while his daughters cowered under a blanket in their room was one of the biggest secrets of all.

A morning carriage ride through the park with the Earl of Radcliffe and no one to chaperone her but the driver was a mark on her reputation that Kitty was willing to risk. But being renowned throughout the *ton* as the offspring of a murderous drunkard? That was a scandal of gargantuan proportions. No gentleman worth his money would want to be associated with such a family.

She didn't want to be associated with such a family.

And if she married William, she wouldn't have to be. If she married William, she could start fresh and leave her past behind. If she married William, she could be the grand lady she'd always envisioned. Which meant, for the indeterminable future, she needed to be on her very *best* behavior.

No losing her temper.

No catty remarks.

Most importantly of all, no more passionate encounters in the parlor.

If she was going to be a countess, then she needed to act like one, as it was evident that her future husband was a man who appreciated rules and decorum, or else he wouldn't have asked to meet her father . . . or stopped at a kiss.

Starting now, she was going to be poised.

Starting now, she was going to polite.

Starting now, she was going to be *perfect*.

"You never told me, my lord, what business took you to Boston," she said, demurely folding her hands in her lap as the horses slowed to a walk in order to safely navigate a narrow bridge, their iron-shod hooves clopping loudly on the stone.

"I am considering purchasing a company and moving it to London."

"Moving an entire company across an ocean? That seems like a daunting task."

Sinewy muscles rippled under the fine cut of his ebony tailcoat as he stretched his arms across the top of his seat. "I am not one to be deterred by a challenge, Lady Katherine."

Her lips curved. "A fine attribute, to be sure."

"Indeed."

They both fell quiet as the carriage traveled along at a leisurely pace past a fragrant hedge composed entirely of lilacs. Reaching out, William grasped a violet bloom and twisted it neatly off its branch. Kitty blinked when he held it out to her.

"For me?" she asked, somewhat dumbly.

The corners of his eyes crinkled. "Unless there's someone else sitting across from me."

"I . . . thank you," she said, accepting the gift with fingers that trembled ever so slightly.

It was foolish, to be undone by such a small, insignificant gesture. Men had given flowers to women for as long as courtship had existed. But up until this very moment, they hadn't given them to *her*.

Compliments and kisses?

She'd received both in abundance.

But a flower . . .

This flower, from *this* man . . .

It meant something. Surely it had to mean something. Or else what was the bloody point of anything?

"Thank you," she repeated, cradling the lilac against her chest with all the care of a newborn babe.

"You're very welcome, Lady Katherine."

"Please . . ." She bowed her head to sniff the flower. When she looked up again, it was with a truly genuine smile. Not the kind that she practiced for hours in the mirror to make certain that she didn't show too much of her teeth or that her nose didn't wrinkle or her cheeks didn't bulge. But a smile straight from her heart. "Call me Kitty."

CHAPTER SIX

April 1813

"I AM GOING to kill him," Kitty fumed as she stalked past the piano in the music room, arms crossed tightly below her breasts. It was late afternoon, the sun already halfway dropped in the sky, and the time that she'd expected William home had come and gone hours ago.

Another hour of waiting. An hour of pacing. An hour of tension knotting up inside her belly as she'd rehearsed all of the words that needed to be said before this farce of a marriage went on another day.

I've had enough.
We both know this is over.
Neither of us is happy.
Why prolong the inevitable longer than we must?

She'd *planned* to discuss their divorce more than a week ago, but then she'd brought Jack home with her instead. The general chaos and upheaval that followed had quelled any conversations regarding their separation. After things had—somewhat—settled down, she'd woken yesterday determined to broach the topic with William over breakfast. But the letter on her dressing table, written in her husband's neat, steady penmanship, had promptly ruined any such plan.

> *My Dear Lady Radcliffe,*
>
> *A new business opportunity calls me away to a buckle factory in Bedford. If all negotiations go accordingly, I should return by breakfast tomorrow morning.*
>
> *Yours,*
> *William*

A buckle factory.

He'd left her for a *buckle* factory.

She shouldn't have been surprised. She certainly shouldn't have been hurt. And it only served to further heighten her annoyance that she was both.

"Kill who?" Jack asked, glancing up from where she was crouched in front of the door in a pair of trousers and a shirt that Kitty had borrowed from one of the maids who had a son around Jack's age and size. She had already sent Jack's measurements to the modiste. A full wardrobe was expected to be delivered by end of the day filled with all of the garments a girl of Jack's age *should* have been wearing. "And can I watch?"

"William, my husband, and no, you may not." *It wouldn't be wise to have any witnesses.* Her eyes narrowed. "What are you doing over there?"

"Practicin'."

"Doing what?"

"Pickin' a lock."

"Picking a—stop that at once!" she exclaimed, throwing her hands in the air. Heavens, she'd known children were exhausting from Lady Roanoke's dreadful pallor after having three of them, but she had never imagined that being a mother would be *this* exhausting. It didn't help that she was raising a future criminal.

Not, she corrected herself with a frown, that any formal commitment had been made pertaining to Jack's future. And she wasn't *really* her mother (if that were the case, she'd have already hired an army of governesses). But she had grown inordinately fond of the little wretch over the past week and a half. Most likely due to the fact that she'd needed to focus her attention on someone other than William and all of the ways a person could be killed without arousing suspicion.

At the moment, she was leaning toward a dash of crushed hemlock in his coffee. From what she'd read, it was quite painful. Agonizing, even.

It sounded delightful.

"If you're practicing anything, it should be your embroidery," she told Jack. "A lady of good breeding is expected to be well versed in the art of embellishing a handkerchief, bonnet, or linen."

Jack scuffed the soles of her new shoes along the polished hardwood floor as she sulked her way to the nearest chair and slumped into it. "My mum never told me who my father is and I don't have a bonnet. Just my lucky hat."

"Oh, I had that thrown out."

"*Ye threw out my lucky hat?*"

"It stank to high heaven. Besides, girls do not wear hats, they wear bonnets. Or caps. Or turbans. Like this," Kitty said, pointing at the fabric wound around the crown of her head and adorned with a trio of dyed ostrich feathers that waved back and forth as she went to the front window for the hundredth time and searched in vain for William's carriage. A carriage that should have, per his letter, returned nearly eight hours ago. Now it was closer to dinner than breakfast, and her patience had officially reached its breaking point.

"That's ugly," Jack huffed from behind her. "I want my hat back."

"I am sorry to say that's not possible." *And neither*, she added silently, *is the timely return of my husband.*

Why did he bother telling her that he was leaving at all? To pretend that he cared? For what purpose? He didn't love her. She sincerely doubted he ever had. Love—true love, lasting love—

wasn't supposed to hurt this much. It shouldn't have hurt at all.

But it did.

It was a large, constant, gaping hole inside of her that she couldn't fill. No matter how many useless pieces of jewelry she bought. No matter how many times she was introduced as the Countess of Radcliffe. No matter how many houses she could call her own. How painfully ironic that she had everything she'd ever wanted . . . yet the one thing that she'd never claimed to want—her husband's love—was what she secretly yearned for most of all.

The bastard.

Hemlock was too good for him, she decided, drumming her fingers on the sill. Yes, death by a poisonous plant was a dreadful way to go. One moment you were enjoying your coffee and the next foam was dribbling out your mouth. Terrible, terrible. But it was too quick for her liking. If William was going to die, then she wanted him to suffer as *she* had suffered these past seven months.

Seven months spent being married to a husband who was in love with another woman.

"We're going out," she said abruptly, spinning away from the window with such force that her turban nearly came dislodged.

"Don't want to go anywhere without my lucky hat," Jack grumbled.

"That's unfortunate, because we're leaving. *Now*," she emphasized when her recalcitrant charge didn't move. Ungrateful child. If she'd displayed even an ounce of hesitation when her father gave her a direct order, she would have earned a slap upside the head for her trouble. Just thinking about it made her skull throb. Which was why she generally didn't. Think about it, that was.

All the slaps.

The hits.

Even a punch if Eriam Holden had been in a particularly foul mood.

It got worse, a hundred times worse, after Mara married her

duke and fled the nest. With no older sister to take the blows, Kitty had endured them all herself. She'd courted William whilst hiding bruises, disguising her shameful secret with long gloves and pretty shawls, teetering between a future ripe with possibility and a present infested with rot.

Then along came Lady Alessandra Mountbatten, the woman William had been betrothed to.

The woman William had conveniently forgotten to tell her about.

The woman who was the start of their ruin.

"Jack, *get up*," she said through clenched teeth. "I'm not about to leave you in this house alone for you to steal all the silver."

Jack rolled her eyes. "I wouldn't steal the silver. Too heavy. I'd start with your bracelets."

Kitty's hand clasped reflexively around the circle of pearls she wore on her left wrist. "And that's precisely why you're coming with me."

"Where are we going, anyway?" Jack asked as she trailed behind Kitty into the foyer. Golden sunlight streamed in through the windows on either side of the front door, dust dancing in the early evening glow. Accepting an emerald-green spencer jacket held out to her by an attentive maid, Kitty made fast work of the gold buttons lining the front of the bodice.

"To visit my sister," she said grimly. "The Duchess of South-wick."

⫸⫷

IN A STOPPED carriage a mile outside London's muddy streets and skies filled with coal ash, William inwardly braced himself for what was to come. He could have ordered his driver to turn around and leave. It wasn't too late, and no one would think poorly of him, because no one knew that he was here.

But *he* knew.

He knew all of the wrongs he had committed.

He knew all of the sins he would have to answer for when his judgment came.

And he knew that daffodils laid to rest on a grave was a pitiful substitute for life, but it was all he had left to offer the woman that he'd killed.

Tightly clutching the bouquet of flowers he had bought from a street vendor for two farthings, he climbed stiffly down from the carriage, gave the driver a curt directive to wait, and proceeded through the rusty front gate of a small cemetery.

Misshapen fieldstones stuck up through the earth in crooked rows. The last remaining testaments to people that time and the living's memory had abandoned long ago. Some of the markers had names and dates, but most were worn smooth by the elements, a blank canvas of anonymity guarding a pile of decaying bones.

William went to the left, following the path of his own footsteps from when last he'd visited this sad, sorry little plot of land set back amidst rolling fields and country cottages. A breeze in from the east, blowing the long grasses and stringy weeds that had claimed the cemetery as their own. There was only one headstone that was not partially overgrown. Tall and straight, it stood slightly away from the rest. Guilt, as familiar as it was bitter tasting, lodged itself in his throat as he knelt down and read the letters engraved across the fieldstone that he'd ordered the mason to polish smooth before carving his betrothed's name upon it.

Alessandra Louisa Mountbatten
April 29, 1792
September 05, 1811
Much beloved daughter

A shoot of milk thistle was beginning to grow in front of the gravestone. He yanked it out without mercy, ignored the twinge of pain when a thorn pierced his glove, and tossed it aside. Blood welled on the pad of his thumb, seeping through the leather, and that, too, was ignored. What was a drop of red when he'd found Alessandra in an ocean of it?

Stop, he ordered himself, as he'd already learned the hard way that thinking of that night did nothing but bring on more guilt. For what he hadn't done. For the one he hadn't saved. For why he hadn't been there.

It was Alessandra's birthday. There was no need to dwell on her death. That would come in September, when the leaves began to change and the wind whipped cold over the gravestones. Today, as penance for what he'd done, he would torture himself with the memory of how she had lived. Or at least, the time during which he had known her.

Alessandra's grandfather, now deceased, had been a close friend of his grandfather, and long before she or William were ever born, the two men had conspired to join their families through marriage.

It should have been a simple enough affair. Lord Mountbatten had a daughter, and the Duke of Cumberland had a son. Two sons, really, except his direct heir was the only one he cared about. But then on the eve of the wedding, the Mountbatten heiress ran away with an actor, much to the general annoyance of Cumberland and the embarrassment of Mountbatten. The matter was never discussed again... until the heiress unexpectedly returned, sixteen years later, with a daughter of her own.

So their plan was revived and the daughter was promptly betrothed to be married to William's uncle, as her mother had been before her, on the day she came of age. William's uncle, who had always been more interested in racing and gambling than finding a bride, didn't care enough to object, but right before they were finally to be wed, his uncle died. With William's father already married, the only male heir Cumberland now had left to offer was his grandson. So the plan shifted again.

At first, William was resistant to the idea of marrying a woman he knew nothing about. A woman who had been promised to his uncle, until a short while ago. But unlike his father, he took his duty as heir to a dukedom quite seriously. Having failed to win the approval of his parents—you couldn't win what was never offered—he was loathe to disappoint his grandfather. And so he agreed, with stoic reluctance, to marry Lady Alessandra Mountbatten.

A meeting was promptly arranged. In private, of course, as Alessandra was still officially in mourning for her dead fiancé, his uncle. The irony of which was not lost on William as he'd been ushered into the Mountbatten drawing room and was formally introduced to his new betrothed.

His first impression of his bride-to-be was not a necessarily favorable one.

Cloaked in black from head to toe, Lady Alessandra had appeared more like a pale wraith than a blushing bride as she'd curtsied before him. In spite of her undeniable physical beauty—ebony hair, delicate features, blue doe eyes behind a veil of wispy obsidian—there was a certain hollow quality about her. A brittleness that extended beyond grief.

When their gazes met, he found hers to be flat and discomfortingly empty. And while he hadn't expected love at first sight (such a foolish notion was reserved for the pages of Byron and Shakespeare), he found himself searching for *some* kind of a connection as they took a turn around the room while their grandfathers watched from a distance. A mutual agreeableness, if nothing else. Except there was nothing agreeable to be seen in the wan, apathetic creature clinging listlessly to his arm.

Still, he understood duty.

The weight of it.

The burden.

His ancestors had fought bloody battles to win the lands that his family now took for granted. If they could do that, then surely he could marry a pretty young woman and produce a male heir. Besides, was it truly any great surprise that Alessandra was behaving in such a way? The poor thing had been betrothed to a man twice her age and was now promised to a total stranger, shifted from one lord to another like a piece of common chattel.

Never mind the rumors that the Mountbattens were . . . odd.

Or that Alessandra's mother was said to have taken her own life.

If the Duke of Cumberland found her suitable enough to marry his only grandson, then she was suitable. That was that.

As they passed by a wall of books, William asked if he could fetch her a glass of lemonade. On either side of the towering shelves, sash windows guarded against a wet, dreary day while inside the drawing room a roaring fire caused an uncomfortable trickle of sweat to drip between the blades of his shoulders. His cravat felt unnaturally tight, and the toes of his boots pinched; tiny discomforts magnified a thousandfold by the tension that hung in the air, heavy and sickly sweet.

"No, thank you," Alessandra replied, her voice as feeble and listless as the rest of her. "I am not thirsty. If you wouldn't mind, I'd like to sit for a while. I did not sleep well, and I find myself on the brink of exhaustion."

William didn't doubt it. His future wife—how strange, to think of her that way . . . to think of *any* woman that way after having been thoroughly enjoying the life of bachelor until a week ago—appeared to be one breath away from collapsing in a heap of black muslin. He carefully guided her over to a matching set of armchairs upholstered in garish pink velvet and, resisting the urge to glance at the longcase clock in the corner, sat down across from her.

"How are you finding the weather?" he asked after a moment of silence that threatened to stretch into an eternity. A servant materialized with a pitcher of lemonade and while Alessandra once again declined, he nodded to indicate he'd like a drink. Preferably a drink far stronger than water and lemons, but there would be time for brandy later. Now, he had a fiancée to get to know.

Women were not foreign concepts to him. As a healthy,

handsome, virile man with a title attached to his name, he'd never been short of feminine attention. But any previous relationships he'd had were solely of a sexual nature, one-night affairs that had ended in the morning or mistresses that had lasted the course of a few months. Aside from instructing his valet on where to deliver jewelry, communication hadn't been a concept worth exploring. But a wife was different. A wife was a permanent fixture. Someone around whom he would plan his life. Someone who would become the mother of his children.

Except as he contemplated Alessandra, slouched in her seat staring aimlessly at the ceiling, he wondered if he'd trust her to raise a pet goldfish, let alone a baby.

"My lady... Alessandra..." He waited for her to look at him. "I understand that this must be a difficult transition for you. Having expected to marry my uncle, and then finding yourself engaged to me. But I shall endeavor to be a good husband to you. You needn't worry on that account."

"Worry?" Her fingers stopped tapping. "Oh, I'm not worried, Lord Radcliffe. I am ecstatic."

He frowned, taken aback. "You are?"

"Yes. Yes, yes." Her eyes took on an unnatural, eerie glint. Like a film of brackish water over a flat pond. "I dreamt of you, Lord Radcliffe. We were dancing. Dancing. *Dancing.*"

From the corner of his eye, William saw Mountbatten rise from his chair. "Alessandra," he began, lines of concern bracketing the corners of his mouth. "Alessandra—"

"Dancing," she continued, mumbling the word like a chant as she spilled clumsily to her feet and began to turn in a circle. "Dancing. *Dancing.* DANCING!"

"My dear, that is enough," Mountbatten said sharply.

"Dancing. We were dancing. Dancing—"

"*Enough.*" He grabbed his granddaughter's wrist and yanked her arm down. Alessandra shrieked and William winced, as the pitch of her voice seemed high enough to shatter his glass of lemonade.

"Grandfather?" She stopped all movement all at once; a marionette whose strings had been cut. "When did you get here?"

Mountbatten whispered something unintelligible in her ear that caused her eyes to widen and her lips to part. She glanced past her father at William, smiled, and then without another word turned on her heel and flounced out of the room.

"You'll have to excuse my granddaughter," said Mountbatten. "On occasion, she is prone to airs of... excess. A trait she inherited from her mother, I'm afraid. Think nothing of it."

Over the course of the next few weeks, Alessandra's behavior—her "airs of excess"—became increasingly erratic. During a walk around the garden, she threw herself on the ground and refused to move unless William made the sun disappear, a feat he managed by draping his coat over her head and ushering her inside where she demanded all of the curtains be drawn.

On a short ride through the park, she went into a panic and claimed the horses were dragons. Had William not stopped her, she would have opened the door and jumped out, seriously injuring herself.

Then there were the five days that he could not pay her a visit at all, as she was stricken by a mysterious illness that prevented her from summoning the energy to even get out of bed. In lieu of a visit, she sent him a letter, but the words were nonsensical and the sentences rambling.

Despite Mountbatten's repeated claims to the contrary, it was clear that Alessandra was not only mentally unwell, but unfit for marriage. Her fits of hysteria followed by periods of severe catatonia made it impossible for William to conduct a normal courtship. But when he raised his concerns to his grandfather, he was brushed away.

"She's a female," said the duke. "Show me a completely sane female and I'll buy you an oceanfront townhouse in the Austrian Empire. That's just how they are, William. Best get used to it."

For the sake of duty, William tried.

But for the sake of honor, he could not marry a woman

whose mind was so obviously fractured.

On the eve of his wedding, he arranged for an audience with his grandfather. And while the Duke of Cumberland looked on with marked disapproval, he explained that he and Alessandra would not be wed, but neither would he end the engagement, which would merely free Mountbatten to foist his granddaughter off on another unsuspecting lord, one who perhaps wouldn't take her well-being into consideration. Instead, he was taking her to a private estate in the country. An estate with caretakers and doctors that discreetly watched over the troubled offspring of well-to-do families.

It wasn't an asylum—he would never commit Alessandra to such a horrid place. But it was a home where she could rest, and hopefully get better, and not have to worry that her maidenhood would be traded away in a contract that would never serve her best interests.

"Mountbatten will be furious," said the duke. "This will be the end of a decades-long friendship. You've disappointed me, William."

"And I'm sorry for that," he acknowledged stiffly. "But I would be sorrier if I went through with a farce of a marriage to a woman incapable of comprehending the vows she was committing herself to. Lady Alessandra doesn't know what season it is on any given day. You know that as well as Mountbatten. And you had to have known that when she was betrothed to my uncle. So I, too, find myself disappointed. In the man that I thought you were and the grandfather I have spent my life idolizing."

The next morning, he accompanied Alessandra to Kilmister Park. She hummed to herself for the entirety of the five-hour carriage ride, and when it was time to disembark, she stunned him by leaning forward, pressing her mouth close to his ear, and whispering, "Thank you."

She was still humming when two nursemaids dressed in white ushered her inside.

"You'll receive a letter once per month with a report on her progress." The lead doctor, a tall, serious man by the name of Dr. Bainbridge, clasped William's hand in a firm shake. "I make no promises in cases such as these. When the ailment is inherited, as this appears to be, we're often left to manage the patient as best we can with no assurances of improvement. But I *can* assure you that Lady Alessandra will be comfortable here, and she will be safe. You may visit whenever you wish, day or night, to see for yourself. While patients are not permitted to leave without prior approval, visitors may come and go as they please."

"I don't want her to be subjected to any painful treatments."

The doctor's mouth thinned beneath the waxed bridge of his moustache. "I've long studied the effects of bloodletting, purgatives, and the like. The results are abhorrent and are the main reason why my colleague and I founded Kilmister Park. Our patients respond best to a calm routine, empathetic care, and therapies that range from music to art to gardening. Your betrothed will be looked after with the utmost respect and consideration for her delicate state."

By all accounts, and as per the letters William received like clockwork at the end of each month, that was exactly what occurred. Once he was satisfied that Alessandra was settled into her new surroundings, he left London for Boston on a nine-month business venture that took him away from Mountbatten, away from the duke, away from his father, and away from any gossip. When he returned, he went first to visit Alessandra and found her to be in remarkably good health . . . with absolutely no memory of who he was.

"I like it here," she told him, striking the ground with her bare foot to propel her swing higher. They were outside in the garden, where the nursemaids told her that Alessandra preferred to spend most of her afternoons. "The people are very nice, and the food is delicious. Especially the rose water macaroons. Rose. Toes." Giggling, she swiveled her ankle. "Snows. Foes. El*bows* . . ."

She was still rhyming when William took his leave. He'd have liked to retreat to Radcliffe Park, his newly inherited 200-

acre estate in Hampshire, but a fresh London Season was calling, and as the Earl of Radcliffe, he was obligated to answer. After so much turmoil—his uncle's unexpected death coupled with his father's inheritance and subsequent gambling debts—the Colborne family needed a responsible representative.

Thankfully, the *ton* was unaware of his and Alessandra's betrothment. It was assumed she'd gone on extended holiday to mourn the death of the late Marquess of Kentwood and no one in either family had seen fit to disabuse the gossip mongers of their speculation, as it was better for them to think that than to suspect the truth: Alessandra was as mad as her mother and the new Earl of Radcliffe had placed her in a manor for the mentally unwell.

Thus, he presented himself at the fourth ball of the Season as if nothing were amiss, strolling through the perfumed masses and sipping weak champagne as if he were just like any other bachelor in attendance. He warded off mothers keen to foist their daughters upon him whilst catching up with a few male acquaintances and accepted condolences for the passing of his uncle with a nod. Those prying for more information were subsequently ignored.

When the hour struck midnight, he was already looking for the nearest exit. But then, by pure, absolute happenstance, he cast his gaze across the ballroom . . . and he saw her.

A blonde vision in blue.

Their eyes met through the crowd, and in the time it took him to blindly set his champagne flute on a passing tray and make his way to her, William was captivated in a way he'd never been before. Not only interested, but *enthralled*. By her face. By her scent. By the way she purposefully flashed her ankle at him when she dropped into a curtsy. By the throaty vibration of her voice as she offered him her hand and then her name.

"Lady Katherine Holden."

Three words, six syllables, and his life, as he'd known it before, as he knew it then, as he would know it to come, was irrevocably changed.

"I am sorry, Alessandra." More milk thistle, spiny and sharp, stabbed William's knees as he knelt and laid his bouquet of daffodils in front of her grave. If he'd loved her more, if he'd loved Kitty less, then maybe, just maybe . . . but no. That was an impossibility not worth dwelling on, as his love for his wife—as twisted and knotted up as it was—far exceeded whatever pitying affection he'd ever felt for his fiancée.

Still, the guilt remained, gnawing into his marrow with slicing little teeth, constantly reminding him of his failures.

As a grandson.

As a protector.

As a husband.

Setting his jaw, he rose to his feet and went to his carriage.

"To Mayfair, my lord?" asked the driver.

"Yes," he said curtly. "To Mayfair."

To home . . . and to a reckoning seven months in the making.

CHAPTER SEVEN

Duke and Duchess of Southwick's private residence
London, England

"*T*HIS IS WHERE yer sister lives?" Jack gasped. "Bloody 'ell."

"Bring your head in the window," said Kitty as their coach pulled up in front of Mara's palatial London residence. "You're not a dog."

Torchlight encased in glass and set on high posts illuminated the neatly raked stone walkway. Kitty kept a firm grip on her young charge's arm as they went to the front door and were promptly admitted inside by a blank-faced servant dressed in black livery.

"Lady Radcliffe and companion," she informed the servant, "here to see my sister."

"The duke and duchess are having dinner. I'll let Her Grace know of your arrival. This way, please."

The receiving parlor they were brought to was a study in varying shades of blue. After pouring herself a glass of wine from a decanter set on top of a liquor cabinet—and refusing to pour Jack one—Kitty perched on the corner of a chaise longue and waited impatiently for Mara to grant them an audience.

Not too long ago, she'd traveled to her sister's country estate unannounced and discovered Mara in the garden pruning roses with her husband nowhere to be found. But things were markedly different now. Now, the Duke of Southwick was very much a present figure in his wife's life. By Kitty's estimation, they rarely left each other's company. Mara and Ambrose had become the rarest of entities in the *ton*: a married couple in love. And she was happy for her sister. Truly. She was. But did Mara have to have *everything*?

The doting duke.

The beautiful house.

The perfect happily-ever-after.

If not for the fact that green had a tendency to clash with her complexion, Kitty would have been draped in it from head to toe.

At least she had *one* of those three things, she reasoned.

Her manor may not have been as large or grand as this, but it was hardly inconsequential. Then there was Radcliffe Park and a hunting lodge in Scotland, along with a townhouse in Bath—all properties that were head and shoulders above where she'd grown up. Why, then, did she not feel the sense of satisfaction that she'd dreamt of as a little girl looking in a shop window at all the shiny things she could not afford?

Maybe, a sly, unwanted voice intruded, *because happiness does not come from possessions, but from deep within ourselves and the people that we love.*

"Oh, do shut up," she mumbled, taking a sip of her wine.

"What?" Jack asked.

"Nothing. Put that bowl down before you break it."

"I'm not goin' to break anything." Jack tossed the small crystal bowl she was holding into the air and caught it with a grin. "See?"

"If you don't put that down—"

"Kitty!" Breathless and beaming, the Duchess of Southwick entered the parlor. "What a wonderful surprise!"

Love, Kitty noted as she returned her sister's embrace, looked good on Mara. Her cheeks, once pale and wan, were now full and rosy. Her auburn hair was sleek and shiny, her brown eyes bright and sparkling. She was the epitome of health and happiness. By comparison, Kitty felt dowdy and, well, *plain*. A strange sensation, to be sure, as the role of the ordinary, forgettable sister had traditionally been relegated to Mara.

"And who is this?" Mara asked, turning to Jack with an expectant smile. A smile that dimmed with uncertainty when Jack promptly tucked the crystal bowl behind her back.

"I wasn't stealing nothin'."

Kitty sighed and gave a vague twirl of her wrist as she flopped onto a chaise longue. "Your Grace, may I present Miss Jack I-Don't-Know-Her-Last-Name."

"Don't have one," Jack provided helpfully.

"She doesn't have one. Jack, meet my sister, the Duchess of Southwick." Kitty paused. "This is the part where you curtsy."

"Don't know how to curtsy."

Kitty cast her gaze heavenward. "She doesn't know how to curtsy."

"I . . ." Mara's gaze went back and forth between them, "I don't completely understand."

"That makes two of us," Kitty muttered into her wine. Finishing off her first glass, she rose from her seat to pour another. "I met Jack in Winslow Park when she attempted to rob me."

"It was just a *tiny* robbery."

"As I've a great deal of affection for my jewelry," Kitty continued on, ignoring Jack, "I chased the little miscreant down and took back what was mine. Then I invited her to stay with me—temporarily, that is—as she hasn't anywhere else to go. But given her propensity for taking what doesn't belong to her, I dare not leave her unaccompanied."

Mara blinked. "That's . . . that's very kind of you, Kitty. Are you feeling well?"

"Are you implying that because I've done a good deed I must be ill?"

"Sounds like it to me," Jack said cheerfully. She gave the bowl another toss into the air... but this time her reflexes weren't quite as quick. "Oops," she said, sucking in a breath when it struck the ground and cleaved in two.

"Jack—"

"It's all right," Mara said hastily. "It's only a bowl. I'll have a maid clean it up. And Kitty, I'm sorry, that's not what I was implying. It is very kind of you to be providing for a child in need. Very kind. Particularly one who tried to rob you."

"Thank you," Kitty sniffed. Then she pressed the back of her hand to the middle of her forehead. "Maybe I *am* ill. It would explain why I've been feeling out of sorts lately." She sipped her wine, then carried the glass over to a cabinet filled with an assortment of porcelain swan figurines. "These are pretty."

"They belonged to Ambrose's grandmother." Sweeping her skirts to the side, Mara sat on the chaise longue that Kitty had left. "I'm glad you're here. I have been meaning to pay a call, but things have been a whirlwind since we got to town."

"Time flies when you're in bed," Kitty said dryly.

"When I'm in... oh. *Oh.*" Mara's cheeks blazed with strips of pink. "Yes, Ambrose and I... we... erm... I can't discuss *that*. There's a child present. But I am pleased to report that our relationship has blossomed. We've never gotten on better. Which leads me to ask how you and William are faring?"

"We're not buttering each other's bread every night like you and your husband, if that's what you're inquiring after. Although we did have a satisfying go round last week."

"*Kitty!*" exclaimed Mara, darting a glance at Jack who had found a platter of cheese on a side buffet and was happily stuffing her face. "You're going to have to curb your language now that you've a young, impressionable charge to care for. Being a guardian is no small responsibility."

"Don't worry about me," Jack chimed in around a mouthful of dairy. "I know all about blowin' the gronsils. Takin' a flyer. Makin' a lobster kettle. Havin' a stitch."

"That's enough. We wouldn't want to upset my older, impressionable sister." Kitty hid her smirk behind the rim of her wineglass. "But if you're asking if I've changed my mind about the divorce, Mara, my answer is no."

Mara's blush drained into a frown. "Surely you and William could figure out some type of reconciliation. You adored each other when you were first married."

"How would you know?" Kitty said, more sharply than she'd intended. "You weren't around. You left London when the ink on your marriage certificate was still wet."

"I was asked to leave by Ambrose," Mara returned quietly. "You know that."

Yes, Kitty did.

In her head, logically, she knew Mara's banishment to Southwick Castle had not been of her own making. But in her heart, the wound of being abandoned by the only person she had ever trusted not to hurt her remained as fresh as the day it'd been scored into her flesh.

Mara was supposed to always be there for her. That was the pact they'd made when they were cowering together under the bed while their father bellowed downstairs. And Mara was. She *was* there. For that, Kitty would forever be grateful. But then, with little warning and no time to prepare, her sister was gone. Her sister was gone, and she was trapped in a house alone with no one to stand between her and the monster that prowled at night.

She could still hear them—the footsteps, heavy on the stairs.

She could hear the sound of her own heartbeat pounding in her chest.

The terrible creak of the door when it swung inward on rusty hinges.

The labored breaths of her father as he'd stared at her.

The fear that had crinkled in her throat like broken glass while she'd waited to see if he would advance toward her bed or retreat into the hallway.

For a year, she'd lived like that. For a year, she'd waited for the worst to happen. And when she was finally rescued, when the monster was finally slain, it wasn't Mara who wielded the bloody knife.

It was William.

"I'm glad that you and your husband are happy, Mara. No one deserves a happily-ever-after more than you."

"But," said Mara, saying aloud the word that Kitty had left unspoken.

"But what worked to fix your marriage is not going to fix mine. William and I . . ." Trailing off, she opened the cabinet door and selected a swan with a crown on its head. "William and I are different. We were forged in fire, but that type of heat is not sustainable. Especially when another person is draining away all of the oxygen."

"I'm confused. Are you saying that William is guilty of an affair?"

On a short, bitter laugh, Kitty returned the swan to its rightful place and turned to regard her sister with an arched brow. "An affair I would welcome, as there's no woman who could compare with me. No *living* woman, that is," she corrected. "But Alessandra isn't alive, and no matter how hard I try or what I do, even I cannot compete with the dead."

"Lady Alessandra Mountbatten?" Mara bit her lip at Kitty's curt nod. "I remember hearing about her, even all the way at Southwick Castle. Such a tragedy, what occurred. I knew there was some connection between the Mountbattens and the Colbornes, but I didn't realize it had anything to do with Lord Radcliffe. Admittedly, I'm not one to pay attention to gossip."

Kitty tilted her head, drained what remained of her wine, and set the glass on top of the cabinet. "I didn't know there was a connection either, until Alessandra appeared on my doorstep in her nightdress and claimed that I'd stolen William from her. It's why we broke off our initial courtship."

"You told me you ended things because William had to travel for business and he wasn't sure how long he would be gone, or if you wanted to wait."

"That," Kitty agreed, "and Alessandra trying to plunge a paper knife into my neck."

"Spectacular," Jack grinned.

Mara's reaction was notably less enthusiastic.

"*Katherine*," her sister gasped. "I—I had no idea. Why didn't you tell me?"

Why hadn't she?

It was a question Kitty had asked herself numerous times.

At first, the shock of it all—and what happened after—was enough to stun her into silence. Then there was the fact that Mara was newly wed, and why would she darken her sister's door with her own problems? Problems of heartache, betrayal, anger, and loss. Thus, when Mara had inquired via letter how her courtship was progressing, she'd glossed over the messier details and written simply that she and Lord Radcliffe had ended things amicably as he was headed across the Atlantic to pursue a merger. Except the merger was here, in London, and there was nothing amicable about the way their courtship had ended.

"It was raining." She considered pouring a third glass of wine, but as her head was already fuzzy and her tongue loose, decided against it. Walking to the chaise longue, she sat beside her sister and gazed intently at a painting on the wall. "It was raining, and it was early, and I was woken by a loud pounding on the door . . ."

Chapter Eight

June 1811
32b Canary Street
London, England

KNOCK. KNOCK. KNOCK.

The sound of someone slamming their fist against the door was loud enough to wake the dead. Kitty groaned and threw an arm across her face as the offensive noise roused her from a deep sleep. She'd been up past midnight, attending a play with William and his visiting great-aunt, Helen, who had nodded off after the first act, leaving her and William to pay closer attention to each other than the actors prancing across the stage.

A slow, leisurely smile crossed her lips as she trailed her fingers fondly along the side of her neck where his whiskers had left a light brush burn on her sensitive skin. She had another red mark above her left breast, and a third on the inside of her right knee. Testaments to a passion that even loud snoring hadn't been able to detract from.

Over the past six weeks, they'd hardly been able to keep their hands off each other. A morning stroll around Vauxhall Gardens was practically an invitation for a clandestine kiss behind a fountain. An afternoon carriage ride through Hyde Park was a wonderful opportunity for petting below the waist. And three nights ago, at the Gloucester Ball, their desire had nearly spilled into outright lovemaking when William followed her into the library.

She wouldn't have minded if it had. In her mind, she and William were practically engaged, and that was as good a reason to lose her virginity as any. Love—an emotion she held in the lowest regard—was a second reason, and much to her surprise, she *did* love William. He was handsome, he was titled, and his kisses made her toes curl. But more than that, he was kind. He was thoughtful. He was considerate of her feelings. He was, to put it plainly, *nice* to her. And she was soaking up all of that niceness with the vigor of a flower in the rain after a long hard drought. However, if that was him rattling the windowpanes at half past eight (a horrid hour, to be sure), she might have to seriously consider whether that love came with caveats.

She passed her father's bedchamber. The door was ajar and a quick peek revealed that Eriam was unconscious half on the floor and half on the bed, an empty bottle of rum tucked lovingly under his chin. Disgust rose within her and she battled it back as she made her way downstairs, stepping around piles of clothing and more empty bottles, some of them broken, as she went. The house hadn't seen a maid for the better part of a month. The cook was gone. So was the butler. Even the footman, a pock-scarred lecher who had liked to ogle her breasts when he thought she wasn't paying attention had finally gone. Mara, the only thread holding the Holden family together, had married her dream duke, gone off to her fancy estate in the country, and in the ashes of her absence, the house had crumbled in on itself.

Kitty had considered writing to her sister and asking for money a dozen times, but pride stayed her quill. If Mara could escape this hellhole of a life—shy, mousy Mara—then surely she could, too. And she was almost there. All she needed was for William to propose, and she'd start planning the wedding. She already had September picked out. Before the first leaves began to fall, she'd be the new Countess of Radcliffe. Then all of this—the secondhand clothes, the glass jewelry, the dust, the dirt, the disgust—would be but a distant memory.

But first, she needed to answer the door.

"I am *coming*," she called out when the pounding increased. Drawing a shawl around her shoulders, she wrenched the brass knob on an impatient huff of breath—and froze at the sight of the person who awaited her on the stoop. Not William, as she'd assumed, nor a creditor coming to collect money that her father didn't have, but a woman. A woman around her age, wearing nothing more than a white nightdress that was stained brown at the bottom with mud. Her hair, black and tangled, lay strewn around narrow, bony shoulders. Cornflower blue eyes dominated a pale countenance with hollow cheeks carved straight out of the bone and lips that were red and chapped.

She wasn't wearing any shoes.

"Who are you?" Kitty asked, not unkindly, as it was clear that the woman was in some sort of distress. Muffling a yawn, she laid her head against the edge of the doorframe. "Can I help you? I fear you may have the wrong address. If you're looking for—"

"Who are *you?*" the woman parroted back, and Kitty felt some of her kindness slip away.

"I'm not sure that's any of your business," she said, straightening. "In case you haven't noticed the time, it's early. I should be in bed. You should be in bed." A frown touched the corners of her lips. "You should also find your shoes."

"You know him." The cornflower blue eyes gleamed unnaturally in the morning gloom of a gray, overcast day that hadn't yet decided if it was going to rain or shine. "You know him. I know that you know him. I know that you do."

"Know *who?* If this is some ploy to get money, I'm afraid you're wasting your unremarkable acting skills." Kitty had taken pains—great, enormous pains—to conceal the dire straits of her financial situation to every person, horse, and mouse in the *ton*, but she felt relatively safe sharing her secret with a lunatic. "We haven't any. Not even a spare shilling. So if you'll be on your way—"

"William is *mine*." The woman shoved into the door with a shocking amount of strength given her frail physique. It caught Kitty on her hip as it swung inward, sending her stumbling back, arms wind-milling for balance. The woman followed her into the foyer, her eyes uncannily light, her steps slow and predatory, and a sliver of fear sliced through Kitty's annoyance as she found herself continuing to back away.

"Now see here," she began, placing her hands in front of her to ward off the woman's steady advance while they turned in a circle in the middle of the small, cramped hall. "I have no idea who you are or what your connection is to William, but you cannot just barge into a stranger's house without an invitation! If you don't leave, I'll . . . I'll scream!"

The woman stopped, and Kitty's chest rose with a sigh of relief. A sigh of relief that lodged itself into her throat like a hook when the woman's head canted to the side and began to *tick, tick, tick* in a clock-like motion.

"They scream at night. It's loud." Her bottom lip jutted out in a pout. "I don't like the loud."

"Who *are* you?" Kitty demanded, even though part of her was quite sure she didn't want to know the answer.

The ticking ceased. A strange quiet unraveled across her face; a busy painting being covered in white so that the artist could start anew. "I am Lady Alessandra Mountbatten, Lord William Radcliffe's betrothed. Who are *you*?"

※※※※

As a habitually early riser, William was already awake and half-dressed when Stevens came to his door.

"Someone is here to see you, my lord."

"At this hour?" William knotted his cravat and slid his arms into a burgundy tailcoat perfectly cut to his broad frame. "Who is it?"

"He did not give me his name, only his calling card. He said that it was urgent he speak with you and is pacing in the front parlor." Stevens held out a small rectangular piece of paper folded in half and sealed with a dot of blue wax.

Brows pinching slightly, William took the card and slid his thumbnail under the wax to pry it open.

> *Dr. Charles Bainbridge*
> *Kilmister Park*

He looked immediately up at Stevens. "The front parlor?"

"Yes, my lord. Would you like me to—"

But William was already shouldering past his valet in his haste to get downstairs and find out why the devil Dr. Bainbridge was in house before breakfast had been served. He'd last heard from the good doctor via a monthly letter updating him on Alessandra's progress. Not that there was much progress to be had. Alessandra remained more or less the same as when he had first brought her to Kilmister Park. Some days, Dr. Bainbridge wrote, she appeared more coherent. Other days she held rigorous conversations with a tree. But there had been nothing of note in his latest recounting of her daily activities. Certainly nothing that would warrant a personal visit at such an hour.

"Dr. Bainbridge." With discretion in mind, William made sure to close the door behind him before proceeding across the parlor to shake the doctor's hand. "How can I help you?"

Visibly distraught, Dr. Bainbridge pulled on the tips of his moustache. "It's Alessandra."

"What about her? Is she ill? Or injured?"

"She's . . . she's missing, Lord Radcliffe."

"*Missing?*" Absurdly, William's gaze traveled around the room, as if he might find Alessandra lurking behind a sofa. "For how long?"

Dr. Bainbridge pulled harder on his moustache. "Four days."

"Four *days*?" he said incredulously. "And I'm only hearing about this now?"

"We had hoped to recover her without incident. It's not unusual for patients to hide around the grounds or even in the manor itself. But after an exhaustive search, it has become apparent that Lady Alessandra is no longer at Kilmister Park. After questioning the staff, I have some reason to think that she may be here, in London. Gossip travels, Lord Radcliffe. One of our maids believes that Lady Alessandra may have overhead her talking about your burgeoning courtship with a Lady Katherine Holden."

Kitty.

William's blood ran hot then turned cold as the weight of the doctor's words—and the worry plainly displayed on his face—sank onto his shoulders with the suddenness of an anchor being tossed into the sea. Preoccupied with his growing infatuation (dare he say, even love) for Kitty, he hadn't dwelled on Alessandra as of late. He'd even pushed back a visit in order to take Kitty on a private tour of Vauxhall Gardens. And whenever guilt had threatened to surface, he told himself that Alessandra was content where she was, that his visits might even be a hindrance to her health instead of a help, as his presence was a reminder of a life she no longer lived. Never in a million years had he imagined that Dr. Bainbridge would bloody well *lose* her. Or that she'd somehow travel all the way to London in order to . . . to what? What business could Alessandra have here? And what were the implications if she were seen and her madness discovered? These were questions that her grandfather should have been responsible for answering, but Mountbatten had washed his hands of his granddaughter once it was plain she was of no social or political use to him. It left William charged with the management of a woman that he hardly knew, but if he didn't care for Alessandra, who would?

A human was not a toy to be cast aside once its use had expired. Clearly, it was a lesson that Mountbatten—and his own grandfather, despite how much he admired the duke—had never learned. But William had. For the entirety of his childhood, his parents had made him feel like a second thought. An inconvenience. A nuisance. He'd told himself that he wouldn't do the same thing to Alessandra, and look what had happened the minute his head was turned by a set of soft lips and bright-blue eyes. From the moment Kitty had sauntered into his world, it had been spinning upside down. Katherine Holden was more than he had ever imagined a woman could be and no less than everything he hadn't realized he needed.

She made him laugh. She made him scowl. She was beautiful. She was conceited. She was open with her passion. She was secretive with her emotions. She challenged him. She teased him. She was tantalizingly, unequivocally perfect for him, the countess of his wildest dreams. So he'd lost himself in her. In their courtship. In their stolen moments of desire. And while he was busy doing that, Dr. Bainbridge had lost Alessandra.

"To be honest," the doctor continued, "I had hoped that Lady Alessandra would be here. With you."

William raised a brow. "Why would she be here with me?"

"You *are* her fiancé."

"And you're her bloody doctor!" The leash he kept on his anger loosened a fraction, and Dr. Bainbridge visibly flinched. "I am paying you a not insignificant sum to ensure that her every need is met. That includes her safety. So where the hell is she? Where is Alessandra?"

"I . . ." The doctor's hands waved uselessly. "I am not sure."

"But you have reason to believe that she is here, in London."

"Yes, I do. We have a weekly shipment of supplies that comes directly from a warehouse on the Thames. The driver unloads, spends the night, and then leaves first thing in the morning. It wouldn't have been difficult for her ladyship to stow away on the wagon."

No, it wouldn't have been difficult. Alessandra may have been trapped in her own little world, but she wasn't lacking in intelligence. Which, in some ways, almost made her plight worse. To have the wherewithal to know that she was different, but not the ability to change.

"Have you been to the Mountbatten residence?" he asked.

Dr. Bainbridge nodded. "Yes. Her grandfather hasn't heard from or seen her since before she was admitted to Kilmister Park. He... he was quite firm that he wanted nothing to do with finding her."

Of course not.

William raked a hand through his hair. "If she's not there, and she's not here, then..." His fingers tightened reflexively at the nape of his neck, blunt nails digging into muscle. "Kitty," he breathed. *She's gone to find Kitty.*

"Pardon?"

But William had already left the parlor, slamming the door in his wake.

⋙⋘

"I'M SORRY, BUT you must be confused." *And mad as a hatter,* Kitty added silently as she stared at the frail, increasingly frantic creature occupying the middle of her foyer. "Lord Radcliffe is not betrothed."

"Yes, he is. Me. He is betrothed to *me*." A hysterical note raised Alessandra's voice an octave, causing Kitty to wince at the high, piercing sound. "He is with me. He is mine. He is not yours. He is *mine*."

"Lord Radcliffe and I have been courting for more than a month. If he had a fiancée, I'm sure he would have mentioned it by now." Still, the absolute certainty in the woman's expression gave her pause. That, and she was sure she'd heard the name Alessandra Mountbatten before. She just couldn't place when or where. "I'd like you to leave. I cannot help you."

"Help?" Her girlish giggle made the fine hairs on Kitty's arms lift straight up. "I don't need help. I need you to go away. I need you to go away, because William is mine. Mine. Mine. *Mine.*"

"Need I remind you that you're standing in *my* house." Kitty's shawl slipped to the ground as she drew herself to her full height and pointed imperiously at the door. "If you don't leave this minute, I'll—I'll have a Runner fetched to make you leave." The Bow Street Runners were charged with investigating crimes and apprehending serious criminals, but surely they'd make an exception in this case. "It is obvious that you are not well, Lady Alessandra. Perhaps if you see a doctor—"

"I'm tired of doctors. I don't want any more doctors." Alessandra grabbed her hair, yanking at the tangled nest of black with her fists as she stomped her feet. "I want *William.*"

"Well, you can't have him," Kitty snapped, her patience having reached its end, "because he is going to marry me."

It was the wrong thing to say. She realized that as soon as the words were out of her mouth. It was like waving a red flag in front of a bull or tossing a fish into shark-infested waters.

Dammit, when would she learn to bite her tongue?

"What I meant," she began, lifting her palms in a placating gesture as Alessandra's nostrils flared and her eyes rolled wildly, "is that the William you are referring to and the William that *I* am referring to must be two different men. That is all. It's early. You look tired. Why don't we—"

"NO!" Alessandra shrieked. "NO, NO, NO!"

A glint of silver flying through the air was Kitty's only warning. She ducked instinctively to the side and the paper knife, long and pointy, struck the wall mere inches from where her face had been. Shocked, she knelt to retrieve the weapon, but before she could close her fingers around it, Alessandra barreled into her at full force and they both went tumbling across the rug while the paper knife skidded just out of reach.

"Let ... go ... of ... me," Kitty grunted, sending an elbow flying into Alessandra's stomach and managing to buy herself a few precious moments of freedom. She went straight for the paper knife, but Alessandra jumped onto her back, and as the air left her lungs on a loud *whoosh* it went skittering out of reach yet again. Struggling in earnest, she tried to flip the smaller woman off her, but what Alessandra lacked in sanity she made up for in strength. It was akin to wrestling with a squirrel. If the squirrel weighed seven stone and had a penchant for deadly objects.

Dread pooled in her belly when Alessandra's arm shot past her and they both grappled for the paper knife, twisting this way and that, kicking and scratching. Somehow Kitty found herself flat on her back with Alessandra's bony knees pressing painfully into her hips. Alessandra held the paper knife and she held Alessandra's wrist clamped in a death grip, knowing that if she wavered, if she weakened, Alessandra wouldn't hesitate to bury the sharp point into her neck. And it would not be the first time the floorboards in this hall were stained red with blood.

This was where Kitty's mother had died. Right here, in this very room, after being pushed down the stairs. Mara thought she hadn't seen, but she had. She had crept out of their room, hunched down behind the stairway spindles, and watched with wide, disbelieving eyes as Mara had wept over their mother's lifeless body. Watched as their father, struck sober by his dark deed, had rolled his wife into a rug and carried her out of the house. Watched as Mara had scrubbed at the red until it turned to pink, then to brown, then to nothing.

Their mother's murder was Kitty's first Big Secret. Kept out of fear of what Eriam Holden would do to her and Mara if they ever spoke of what happened that night. Over the years, that fear grew to include what High Society would think of her if they knew she was the daughter of a murderer. A daughter who had shamefully kept her silence instead of having the courage to say the truth. Now fate was making sure that she paid for her sins. By striking her down in the same place where her mother had perished, it was evening the scales. Making right what was wrong.

But Kitty wasn't ready to die.

Not when she finally had so much to live for.

Raising her head, she sank her teeth into Alessandra's wrist. With a howl of pain, Alessandra dropped the paper knife and fell to the side, clutching her arm. Her heart beating wildly, Kitty picked up the paper knife and waved it in front of her while she scrambled to her feet. A row of scratches burned on the side of her neck, and her hair, once plaited in a neat ribbon down the middle of her back, cascaded over her shoulders in a messy waterfall of blonde. She parted her lips, but before she could speak, the door crashed open and William came barreling through.

"*Katherine.*" He stopped short and sized her up in one glance, his brown eyes burning black as he took in the red marks on her ivory skin. "Are you all right?"

"Am I . . . am I all right?" This time it was her voice that shook with a chord of hysteria. "No, no I am decidedly not *all right*. This woman"—she jabbed the paper knife at Alessandra who remained on the floor in crumpled heap, moaning and holding her bleeding wrist—"came in and attacked me! She was blabbering on about how the two of you are engaged. She's clearly insane, and I don't know what asylum she escaped from, but—"

"Alessandra," said William quietly, and Kitty's jaw dropped at the resigned tenor of recognition in his tone. "What have you done?"

"I wanted to see you," Alessandra moaned pitifully. "I wanted to see you and *she*"—she glared at Kitty—"wouldn't let me."

"You tried to *stab* me with a *paper knife!*" Her gaze cut to William as her mind tried to puzzle out the impossible. "She was ranting and raving about being your fiancée. But that cannot be true. Tell me that cannot be true."

"It's . . ." He rubbed the bridge of his nose. "It's complicated."

Kitty sucked in a breath. "What's complicated about it? You either are, or you aren't. You've either lied to me since we met, or you haven't."

"Alessandra and I were betrothed. We—we are betrothed still, I suppose, but none of it was by my choice. I should get her back to Dr. Bainbridge, and then I can explain." He reached for her hand, but Kitty pointed the paper knife at him.

"Don't *touch* me."

His mouth flattened. "Katherine—"

"Get out. Get out, both of you!" she yelled, her chest heaving on a suppressed sob of pure, wretched emotion. "I *never* want to see you *ever* again."

Then she waited.

She waited for him to tell her it was all some kind of cruel jest. She waited for him to pick Alessandra up and toss her out the door. Because this couldn't be happening. This couldn't *really* be happening. Not when she was so close to her happily-ever-after. Not when she was so close to having all she'd ever dreamed of.

Except in her dreams, William wasn't engaged to someone else.

"I'll explain," he repeated gruffly. "When I return, I'll explain everything."

Her hand holding the paper knife fell numbly to her side as she watched him gather Alessandra and escort her out the door. When it clicked into place, the tiny sound loud as a gunshot in the echo of his absence, the tears came, stinging the scratches on her neck as a flood of salty water rained down across her cheeks.

In her dreams, William never broke her heart.

CHAPTER NINE

April 1813
Duke and Duchess of Southwick's private residence
London, England

"AND THEN WHAT happened?" Mara asked, her hands clasped so tightly together in her lap that the blood had leached from her knuckles.

"Aye, don't stop there," Jack chimed in agreement from where she'd settled on the armrest of the chaise longue, pointy chin cupped in the palm of her hand. "What 'appened when William came back? Did ye stab him? I would've stabbed 'im."

"No, I didn't stab him." Kitty rose to her feet and shook out her skirts. "He tried to make his explanation—briefly—and I left London shortly thereafter. Then I married him. Eventually."

Jack's nose wrinkled. "Gross. Why would ye go and do a thing like that?"

"Because she loved him." Mara stood up and placed a comforting hand on her sister's shoulder. "And I'm sure it was nothing more than a large misunderstanding."

"I needed him in order to escape an untenable situation," Kitty corrected. "Love had nothing—love *has* nothing—to do with it. Thus, my desire for a divorce."

"I would've stabbed him. Right here, in the heart." Jack drove a fist into her chest as she dove face first onto the chaise longue. "What happened to the madwoman?" she asked, her voice muffled by the cushions. "Did ye at least stab *her*?"

"Alessandra died two months later," Kitty said curtly. "She took her own life by jumping out a window. Then William went to Boston for a year, and I—"

"You came to Southwick Castle," Mara murmured. "I remember. You said it was because your complexion was in desperate need of fresh country air, but you never made mention of what truly happened between you and Lord Radcliffe. Oh, Kitty. I'm so very—"

"Sorry, yes." She shrugged out of her sister's embrace. "It was all very sorry. For everyone. Alessandra was ill. Her mind . . . it wasn't right. But William knew what he was doing. He knew what he was withholding from me."

"Lord Radcliffe is a good man. I'm sure he had his reasons, and we *all* have our secrets," Mara said with quiet significance. "You still married him. Despite what he'd concealed from you, you still made the choice to marry him. You made vows, Kitty. Before God. Vows that cannot be easily undone."

Kitty gave an indelicate snort. "You're one to talk about vows. If memory serves, you were considering taking a lover not too long ago!"

"You know that's not true," Mara hissed, her cheeks turning the same shade of pink as the climbing roses on the front trellis. "I wasn't going to really take a lover. Not in the way that you're implying. And since resolving our . . . marital relations . . . Ambrose and I have never been happier."

"Not all marital relations can be resolved."

"I wish you'd told me this sooner. I could have helped, or at least provided support." Mara reached out and squeezed her hand. "You are my sister, and I love you."

Part of Kitty wanted to fling her arms around Mara's neck and hold onto her like she'd done when they were little girls. The other part wanted to curl up in a dark, damp cave to lick its wounds like an injured animal.

The animal won.

"Come along, Jack." She slid her hand free of Mara's grasp and turned toward her charge. "It's time to go."

"But I was jest gettin' comfortable," Jack complained as she peeled herself off the chaise longue. Her gaze slid to the half empty decanter on the liquor cabinet. "Can we take that with us?"

"No."

"But—"

"You can stay here if you'd like," Kitty said, starting for the door. "I'm sure they could use another scullery maid."

"Scrub chamber pots? The 'ell I will." Jack sprinted out of the parlor as if her shoes had caught fire, while Kitty hesitated in the threshold.

"I wish that William and I could be like you and Ambrose." She kept her eyes low. "I see how he looks at you. William does not look at me like that. I don't think he can, not with all of the guilt he has inside him from what happened to Alessandra and . . ."

"And?"

"Nothing." She gave a curt shake of her head. "Our marriage contains a ghost, and there isn't room for the three of us. I don't *want* a divorce, Mara. But I need to be free."

"I understand," Mara said softly. "But I would caution you on one aspect."

Her fingers tapped impatiently on the doorframe. "And what's that?"

"Make sure it's your husband you're running from."

⇾⇾⇾⇽⇽⇽

THE HOUSE WAS eerily quiet when William entered the front hall.

That, in and of itself, told him Kitty was not in the residence, a suspicion confirmed shortly by Stevens.

"Her ladyship"—the valet's voice dripped with barely concealed disdain—"left before dinner, my lord. She took that . . . urchin . . . with her."

"You mean Jack?" he asked, handing off his coat and hat to a waiting footman.

"Yes." Stevens's face pinched inward, as if he'd just caught wind of a terrible stench. "*Jack*. Are you aware that yesterday she was caught swinging from the curtains in the drawing room? And the day before that, she used the banister as a slide. A *slide*, my lord."

"Sounds to me like our guest is enjoying herself." To William's bemusement, he had already started to grow somewhat fond of Jack. While their interactions had been limited to a few dinners and one rainy afternoon spent teaching Jack how to play piquet while Kitty had been at the modiste, the wild youth was entertaining (if a bit of a card cheat), and she kept Stevens on his toes. She also seemed to make Kitty happy . . . and that had to count for something, as it was more than he could do.

"At this rate, that wretched child will have the house destroyed by the end of the month," Stevens predicted darkly.

The corners of William's mouth twitched. "Come now, it can't be all that bad. Did the countess give you any indication of when she would return?"

"No, my lord, she did not."

"In that case, I'll retire early."

Flickering candlelight guided him up the stairs to the master bedchamber. Swathed in burgundy wall hangings and dominated by a gargantuan four-poster bed complete with canopy, it was a heavily male dominated space. There was nothing of Kitty in here. Nothing but the memory of her perfume and perhaps a blonde hair under his pillow, left there from their last wanton copulation.

He'd have preferred that she slept by his side. Separate bedrooms were never something that he'd aspired to in his marriage. But the wall between them was tallest at night, and barring an evening rendezvous brought on by lust and wine, the door leading from this bedroom to the next remained closed and locked.

He poured himself a glass of brandy from the decanter beside his bed and began to undress, forgoing a cumbersome nightdress in favor of sleeping in a loose-fitting pair of cotton drawers, leaving his upper body exposed to the balmy spring air nipping in through a partially cracked window. Picking a tome at random from the bookshelf on the far wall, he settled himself on the mattress, took a sip of his drink, and flipped idly to the first chapter to read by candlelight, an ingrained habit that helped him calm his mind and ready it for sleep . . . something that didn't always come easily.

The careless stomp of feet on the stairs alerted him to Kitty's return. His brow creasing, he pointedly turned to the next page, forcing his thoughts to remain within the parameters of the ink and paper propped against raised thighs. In another world, in another marriage, he might have left his room to greet his wife in the hall. Might have welcomed her back with a searing kiss before tossing her over his shoulder and loping off to the chamber they both shared. Might have blown out the candles and peeled off her garments by the light of the moon. Might have laid her out on the bed with her legs dangling off the side and crouched between them, his mouth salivating at the sweet nectar he could already taste on his tongue.

But in this world, in *this* marriage, he merely drank his brandy before turning to the second chapter. And it wasn't what he wanted. It wasn't what he'd bloody well dreamt of after that first night when he kissed Kitty on the terrace. But after everything he'd done . . . after everything he'd done, it was no less than what he deserved.

Abandonment, mistruths, *murder*.

Who the hell was he?

What the hell had he become?

Falling in love with Katherine Holden had brought out his best qualities, but it had also revealed the worst. It had peeled back the protective layers he'd constructed around himself with painstaking care and then stripped them away fully, leaving him raw, exposed, and vulnerable. The three things he abhorred more than anything else.

Vulnerability was weakness.

Weakness was pain.

Hadn't he learned that as a young boy, waiting in vain for his parents to notice him? To approve of him? To *love* him?

When the pain of being ignored and overlooked finally became too much to bear, he'd learned how to lock it away, to hide it within himself and put on a front of cold indifference. A front that Kitty had cracked open wide with her guileless blue eyes and mischievous grin. And just when he'd thought that he had no more need for the vault around his heart, just when he was getting ready to throw away the key that locked the door up tight, he managed to fuck it all the way around.

Not to say *everything* was his fault.

His pretty little wife was not blameless, although he didn't blame her. How could he? How could he when he'd never told her? About Alessandra. About the engagement. About Kilmister Park. About any of it. It had been more convenient to tuck it away. To tell himself that it was all taken care of because he was taking care of it—not because he had to, but because if he hadn't, no one else would.

He'd tucked Alessandra away with one hand and embraced Kitty with the other under the bold, naïve assumption that never the twain would meet. Until they did. Until the woman he vowed that he'd provide for had threatened the woman he wanted to marry. And he had handled it . . . poorly.

He saw that now.

He'd seen it *then*, as it was bloody happening, but he wasn't perfect. He wasn't a saint. He'd made a mistake. He'd mishandled the situation, and by doing so, had done nothing but cause more hurt. To himself. To Kitty. To Alessandra.

Poor Alessandra, whose fractured mind hadn't been able to contemplate a life without him, whose jealousy had burned through what remained of her sanity. Whose bedroom window had shattered when she threw herself against it and plummeted to her grisly end.

Blood and roses.

Her life had ended in blood and roses, while his . . . his had continued on at the pace of a death march.

His parents, oblivious.

His grandfather, on extended holiday.

His secret fiancée, dead.

His relationship with Kitty, ended.

He still remembered, with vivid clarity, the hurt in her eyes when he'd stood on her doorstep in the midst of a drenching rain. His hat in his hand, with water sluicing off his face, he had tried to explain the unexplainable.

"*I'm sorry, I should have told you.*"

"*Yes, we were engaged.*"

"*Yes, I am responsible for her.*"

And then, the worst:

"*I cannot leave her in such a fragile state. When she's better, we can resume our courtship. Until then . . . until then, I should remain close to Kilmister Park.*"

"You shouldn't have kissed me," she'd said as sparks of anger had begun to burn through the hurt in those wide pools of endless blue. "*If you were engaged to her, you shouldn't have kissed me.*"

How could he have disagreed, when it was the truth? Even though he never had any intention of marrying Alessandra, they were still connected. He shouldn't have pursued a courtship with Kitty until the lines were clearly drawn, until the two of them had been clearly separated. He shouldn't have lied to her by omission or presented himself as unencumbered. But he had. He had, because to have *not* kissed Kitty in those whispers of moonlight would have been like turning his back on the fucking sun.

"Alessandra has doctors who can care for her," Kitty had reasoned. *"You don't have to be there."*

"I do," he'd said, even though he knew it wasn't the answer she wanted or would accept. *"I do have to be there."*

"For how long?" She'd glanced over her shoulder into the house and something had flickered in her gaze. Something he'd never seen before, but something he would see in the future: fear. *"How long will I have to wait?"*

"I am not certain," he'd admitted. *"I don't know how long it will take for her to stabilize. I do . . . I do have strong feelings for you, Kitty. I anticipate this courtship blooming into a thing of great significance."*

"Blooming," she had repeated. "Blooming when, William? I won't be a man's second choice."

"You're not my second choice. You're . . ." But when the words wouldn't come—how could he give her words he'd never heard himself?—she'd closed the door in his face, as was her due, and he'd gone to Kilmister Park, as was his.

For weeks, months, he'd worked with Dr. Bainbridge and Alessandra to reach a path forward. He'd done everything in his power to help her understand that while he cared for her and her wellbeing, he did not belong to her. The engagement was over. He was not going to be her husband. He was going to marry someone else—if that someone else would have him. When it appeared Alessandra was making progress, when Dr. Bainbridge assured him that she would not escape again, he got in his carriage—on that fateful September 5th—and he tried to leave . . . until the screams brought him rushing back.

He sent letters off to Alessandra's family and waited for them to arrive before proceeding with a funeral. He sent a letter to Kitty as well, but if she received it, she did not reply.

Finally, after all that could be settled with Alessandra was settled (aside from the gnawing guilt that her grandfather, Mountbatten, did not share), he made haste for London. For the woman he'd left behind in the rain. But Kitty wasn't there. She wasn't *any*where that he could find. So William did the only logical thing he could think of. He'd left one last letter for her in London and then he'd taken his bruised heart back to Boston, where the Americans' relentless entrepreneurial spirit had kept his mind busy for the better part of a year while his soul had hardened. And once twelve months had passed, once the first anniversary of Alessandra's suicide had come and gone, he'd returned to lay flowers on her grave.

Then he'd committed murder.

Jaw clenching, he closed the book he'd been pretending to read and ran his fingers through his hair, disheveling the wheaten strands. After such a tumultuous courtship, had he really expected to have a calm, peaceful marriage? Madness, mayhem, and murder: the building blocks that had started his relationship with Kitty. Now, if she had her way, divorce would end it. And would it truly be that terrible? A legal separation slicing their entwined lives apart. Naturally, the gossip mongers would have a feast. But he'd never concerned himself with what others thought. If he had, his parents' apathy would have crippled him a long time ago.

William looked sharply at the door when it creaked open and Kitty slipped inside. She wore only an ivory dressing robe belted loosely at the waist, exposing the rounded curves of her magnificent breasts to his ravenous gaze. Her nipples, dusky rose in the muted yellow glow, were clearly visible through the sheer fabric of her robe and already erect. A maid had taken the pins from her hair and it swung loose over her shoulders and down her back in a tousled spill of yellow silk. Her eyes were heavy. Her lips slightly parted.

"What are you doing?" he said hoarsely. "It's late, Kitty, and I don't have the energy to fight with you. Not tonight."

"I didn't come here to fight." She closed the door with a subtle nudge of her bare heel and then leaned against it. Her fingers, long and elegant, went to the knot over her left hip . . . and his mouth went dry when she pulled and her robe fell open before slithering to the floor in a pool of white. "I came here for you."

"You don't want me."

A poignant smile briefly shaped her lips. "I've *always* wanted you, William. Even when I shouldn't. Even when I tell myself not to. This"—she tapped the side of her head—"knows better, but this"—her hand trailed slowly down her body, tracing over hill and valley before she touched herself between her thighs—"has never listened. And it doesn't feel like listening tonight."

It was a bad idea.

A bloody *terrible* idea.

Coming together in the cover of darkness wasn't going to fix what was broken in the light. Then again, maybe nothing could fix what was broken. Maybe . . . maybe it was better to simply make do with the shattered pieces. Because as loath as he was to admit his own weakness, having half of Kitty was better than having none of her.

He left the bed and shed his trousers in one fluid motion, revealing a hard cock sprung to attention. Meeting her at the door, he grasped her wrists and yanked them above her head, pinning them to the wood before he took her mouth and devoured it, tongue thrusting boldly between plump lips to lick and savor.

She kissed him back, their passion as wild and sprawling as Scottish heather in the heat of summer.

Abandoning his grip on her arms, he fell to his knees in front of her and nudged her thighs apart. She gasped when he licked the small nub nestled in a bed of dark blonde curls, nails skimming across his scalp before anchoring in dual fistfuls of hair. She nearly ripped out the strands by the roots when he plunged his tongue inside of her, but there was immense pleasure to be found in the haze of pain. Jutting his palms up against the half-moon curve of her hips, he held her fast to the door as he feasted on all that was sweet with a hint of tart. Blackberry filling without the extra measure of sugar.

When her legs quivered, when her toes curled, he continued to ruthlessly plunder and pillage, taking more. Taking *everything* her delectable little body had to give and then some. Only when she wilted on a dreamy sigh, only when his arms were the only thing holding her upright, did he rise to his feet and carry her to the bed.

She squealed when he tossed her on top of it, bouncing harmlessly on the mattress before scrambling to the other side, a half-hearted attempt at escape in a game that they both enjoyed. Snaring her ankle, he pulled her into the middle of the bed and pounced with a low, rumbling growl, nipping her shoulder before flipping her over to stare triumphantly into sapphire-blue eyes burning with desire.

Thick lashes fanning low over to the tops of her cheeks, she stretched her arms above her head, lazily arching her back and drawing his animalistic focus to her stunning breasts.

"Do you want *me*, William?" she purred.

"Yes," he said harshly, muscles tensing as he held himself poised above her.

"Then take me."

So he did. On top of her, with her legs wrapped around his buttocks. Underneath of her, with her sitting astride riding him better than any horse. Behind her, with her round arse pushed flush against his loins and his cock buried to the hilt in wet, velvet heat.

He took her again, and again, in countless ways, in a myriad of positions, always teetering along that razor-sharp edge. Pouring all of himself into all of Katherine. Into the woman that made him gnash his teeth in frustration even as he yearned to hold her close. Into the woman that was the source of all his dreams and the cause of all his nightmares. Into the woman he should have left, who wanted to leave him. But that would mean giving *this* up, and that . . . that, he would never do.

Katherine was *his*, Godammit.

His wife.

His lover.

His nemesis.

Whether she wanted to be or not.

When they finally came, when release rolled like a wave, it consumed them both in a fierce, fiery crash and they collapsed in a breathless heap side by side, Kitty dazed with a wrist draped limply across her temple whilst William lay with a knee raised and an arm crooked under his head.

Reaching blindly for the brandy he'd set aside earlier, he took a sip and then passed the glass to his wife. With a murmur of assent, she sat up just high enough to drink, and one side of his mouth raised in a superior male smirk when she sputtered, wrinkled her adorable nose, and shoved the brandy back into his hand.

"That's not wine."

"No," he agreed before he finished the remaining contents. "It isn't."

Silence reigned, not entirely uncomfortable, and William's eyes began to grow heavy before he felt Kitty stirring beside him.

"Leaving?" he asked, keeping his tone deceptively neutral as she sat up and swung her legs over the side of the bed, her hair tumbling down the middle of her spine in a tangle of curls.

"I sleep better in my own chamber." She started to stand and cast a questioning glance over her shoulder when he leaned sideways and grasped her by the elbow, his fingers wrapping around the delicate web of green veins hovering just below the surface where her pulse fluttered steadily.

"And if I requested that you remain here? With me? Would that be so terrible?"

She turned her head, shielding her countenance from his view. "We've discussed this—"

"No, we haven't. We fuck," he said flatly. "And we fight. There's nothing in between."

"Is *that* so terrible?"

"Is it what you want?" he challenged, holding firm to her arm when she tried to pull it away. "Because I don't."

"What I want is a divorce."

"Yes, I am aware. You've made that abundantly clear. But I'm not letting you go, Katherine."

"Why the bloody hell not?" she asked shrilly. Under the pad of his thumb, her pulse began to race. "You don't love me, William. You married me out of guilt, and I married you to better my situation. We both know it. We may keep our secrets from everyone else, but not from each other."

"You're right."

"Furthermore, I—what?" she broke off, incredulous. "*What did you say?*"

"You're right." It was the first—now the second—time he'd ever spoken those two words aloud to Kitty, words he'd kept compressed down deep, where the *real* truth lived. The truth he didn't share with anyone. Not even himself. "Our courtship was a fucking disaster from the beginning to the end. I wish it had been different. But it wasn't. And we can't change that. *I* can't change what happened to Alessandra, or my part in it. I can't change that I withheld my engagement from you. I can't change that I left you. I can't change what I did to your father. Of course I feel guilty, Kitty." He released her elbow to run his hands across his face. "I killed two people. And before their blood was even dry, I married you. What kind of man does that make me?" Indescribably weary, he closed his eyes and let his head fall against the mahogany headboard with a soft *thud*. "What kind of husband?"

For a moment, there was nothing but quiet in the black behind his eyelids.

The heavy rasp of his breathing.

The creak of the bed.

The pop of a wick as a candle burned low.

"William, you . . ." Kitty's sigh was as light as a snowflake spinning to the frozen ground. "You're not a bad man and you're not a bad husband. I am . . . *aware* that I can be difficult. Selfish. Conceited, certainly. Quick tempered, maybe a little. But I'm not a bad woman. Neither of us are bad people, even after what we've done. But that doesn't mean we're good *together*." She placed her hand on his thigh, fingers spreading across taut muscle. "We shouldn't have married. It was impulsive and reckless. We made a mistake. That's all. A mistake that I am trying to correct."

He opened his eyes to find her staring at him. Not with anger, as was so often the case these past few months, but with compassion. With empathy. With understanding.

All things being equal, he'd have preferred the anger.

"I would give you the moon, if you wanted it," he rasped. "But I won't give you this, Katherine. I can't. There will be no divorce. You won't leave me."

Her eyes flashed before she withdrew her hand. Lifting a corner of the coverlet, she covered her breasts. "Then give me a reason to stay, William. Tell me what I want to hear. What I *have* to hear, if we're to try building anything from this pile of ash."

Love. She wanted words of love, of affirmation and adoration. They were words that he should have been able to give freely. Words that were just that . . . *words*. Spoken in one breath and gone in the next. Except they weren't *just* words. Not to him. Not to the boy who had never heard them himself. And not to the man who didn't think he deserved to feel them.

If he told Kitty he loved her, he would mean it. In his heart. In his head. In the depths of his blackened soul. But to love her, to love her *completely*, would also mean abandoning his guilt. It would mean absolving himself of his sins. Of the crimes he'd committed and the pain he'd inflicted, both on purpose and by accident.

And that . . . that he wasn't ready to do.

"I've given you all that I can. All that I'm capable of." He rubbed the heel of his hand into the center of his chest where his heart remained hard and unyielding. "I care for you, Kitty. Deeply. That will have to be enough."

"But it isn't." She took the coverlet with her as she slid off the bed. "It isn't enough, William. It is never going to *be* enough. I spent my childhood waiting for love from a father incapable of giving anything but slaps and kicks. I won't spend my adulthood doing the same. I refuse."

"I would never hit you," he said, stricken.

"No, you wouldn't. But there are other ways to hurt the people you care about." Her mouth thinned. "You should know that better than anyone."

He gritted his teeth. "Kitty—"

She was already gone.

Chapter Ten

That night, as she tossed and turned and stared at the canopy above her bed, Kitty did her best not to think about that *other* night. The night that had changed everything. The night that had altered the course of her entire life. The night that she made William swear he would never speak of again. The night that she wanted to strike from her memory.

So, naturally, that was the night she thought about.

It was September. A year since Alessandra had died and William had left. The whispers and rumors had mostly dwindled away, but it had taken the whole year. No one knew the entire truth except for William. Not even Kitty. And as he hadn't been present for the past twelve months to dispel the wilder speculation, various stories had twisted and grown like weeds overtaking a rose garden.

After Alessandra died, news of her secret engagement to William was made public knowledge, most likely spread by a servant, or perhaps even Mountbatten himself. Most people assumed—correctly—that the engagement had been arranged by their families, a means for appeasing the Duke of Cumberland after the death of his firstborn heir. Distasteful, perhaps, to marry off one's grandson to the woman his son had been engaged to, and likely that was why it had been kept a secret. But it wasn't unheard of. After that, the gossip became a bit more... farfetched.

Some said William had tossed over Alessandra for Kitty. Others swore it was the other way around. A few slyly implied he'd courted both at once.

But where it got *truly* interesting was with Alessandra's death.

The papers reported that she had followed in her first fiancé's footsteps and perished in a tragic accident. Any specific details were withheld out of respect for the family's wishes, or so that was what the reporter was paid to write. Lord Radcliffe, heartbroken over her passing, had gone to America to mourn in private for an undetermined length of time. His brief courtship with Kitty was not even worthy of an afterthought. And that was that. A messy, sprawling, convoluted story wrapped up in five neat paragraphs and tied with a pretty bow.

Of Alessandra's health, or Kilmister Park, or paper knives, there was no mention.

Anywhere.

But the whispers didn't stop there. The bolder rumors wondered if Lord Radcliffe had anything to do with Alessandra's... accident. By then, most had forgotten about the public sightings of him and Lady Katherine Holden together. But not all. And those who remembered spun tales of the lengths a man would go to in order to have the woman he *really* wanted, not the one his grandfather had told him to marry. But if William had gotten rid of Alessandra to wed Kitty, why had he disappeared to Boston? And why hadn't Kitty gone with him?

Eventually, the whispers lessened. New scandals sprang up. And the messy triangle comprised of Kitty, William, and Alessandra was ignored by those who had bothered to dwell on it at all.

After spending Christmas with Mara at Southwick Castle, Kitty returned to London to prepare herself for a new Season and finding a new beau. Mara had asked—begged, almost—for her to remain, and while she was loath to live with their father, Kitty knew that if she ever wanted to permanently escape him, she would need to find a husband of her own. But no matter how many balls she attended or how many eligible bachelors she danced with, it soon became painfully obvious that none of them were William. Even if she closed her eyes, she was hard pressed to get him out of her head. And her heart... her heart was a torn, bloody mess.

Still, she persisted. She would find someone to replace William. She *had* to.

If not, she genuinely feared what might happen to her... and what her father might do. Most days—weeks, months even—Eriam was lost in his cups and his gambling dens, but on the nights he made it back home, stumbling and slamming doors, Kitty had lain awake, eyes wide, body tense, her door closed and the knife she'd taken from the disaster of a kitchen clutched in her clammy fist.

When summer came, and with it the unbearable stench of horse dung that hung over London in a pungent cloud, she went back to Southwick Castle and found temporary respite with Mara.

"Fine," she said automatically when her sister questioned how their father was. "He's doing fine. He's better since you married. Much better. You needn't worry about me."

She could have told Mara the truth.

She should have.

But then Mara would have insisted that she remain at Southwick Castle, and how was Kitty meant to find a husband there? Nor could Mara accompany her to London, as Ambrose had forbidden her to leave.

Men.

Dung beetles, the lot of them.

Maybe she would have been better off *not* marrying. Maybe she would have been better off letting herself turn into a spinster and playing the part of doting aunt to any children Mara and Ambrose would one day have... if they ever got around to living together.

But she didn't want to live in her sister's shadow. She wanted her *own* light, her own household to manage, and her own family to look after. She wanted... well, she still wanted William, dammit. Even though he'd made it abundantly clear with his long absence that he didn't want her, that he couldn't care less about her, that the time they'd spent together and the kisses they'd shared meant nothing.

Until suddenly, without any warning, there he was. Standing across a crowded ballroom, just like the first time she saw him.

And it was the same—exactly the same—but somehow, completely different. Heart wrenchingly different.

Dangerously splendid in all black, he was a tad leaner than she recalled. His cheekbones were sharper. His jaw harder. But it was him. It was William. Her William. Except he wasn't hers. And before he caught her staring, she'd fled out into the cool, crisp autumn night, the train of her gown sweeping out behind her in a wave of yellow.

Racing down a set of stone steps, she stopped at the bottom, pressing both hands to the base of her throat where her pulse pounded against her clasped fingers as she drew a ragged breath. Above her, the sky was an inky, endless expanse of glittering stars. Below her feet, the crushed gravel pathway was damp with midnight dew. And inside her chest... inside her chest, her traitorous heart beat wildly.

She was never supposed to fall for William.

She was never supposed to be in love with him.

She was never supposed to *miss* him.

He was, from the beginning, a means to escape her father and ensure financial security. He was an avenue to grand country houses and dresses that weren't fraying at the seams. But somewhere along the way, he'd turned into more. And she hated it.

She hated that she loved him.

"Katherine." His voice was velvet over steel as he approached her from behind, his stride steady and even. When he stopped, his shadow overlapped hers, broad shoulders and tapered waist caressing the rounded curves of her silhouette. "I had hoped to see you tonight."

"Here I had hoped to never see you again." The words were out before she could control them, whiplashes of her tongue bred from misery and resentment. "Go away, William."

Please don't go away.

"I was in Boston longer than I anticipated. I tried to find you." His voice roughened. "Before I left, I tried to find you. But you were nowhere to be found."

"I have nothing to say to you."

I'm excellent at hiding from the people who hurt me. I have everything to say to you.

"I thought of you. Every day that I was gone, I thought of you." He reached for her hand and she flinched when their gloves touched before yanking her arm away. "I'm sorry, Kitty."

"For what?" she snapped, glaring fiercely at the climbing roses winding up a tall wooden trellis. The white petals glinted silver in the moonlight. "For not telling me about Alessandra? For lying about your engagement? For leaving England? I'm afraid you'll have to be more specific, William. What is it, exactly, that you're apologizing for?"

"All of it. I am apologizing for all of it, and I—Kitty, won't you look at me? Just look."

But she didn't want to, because as soon as she turned around and let herself drink in the familiar lines of his countenance and the rich brown of his eyes, she'd be helpless to resist him. Gritting her teeth, she shook her head, and William released a short, barking laugh caught somewhere between amusement and frustration.

"Fine. Then I'll say what you wouldn't let me when Alessandra came to London."

"You mean when the woman you forgot to tell me you were betrothed to tried to *stab me*."

"I never wanted to marry her. It was not my choice, but my

grandfather's."

"You could have said no."

"To a duke? Or to the poor, sick girl who was being used as nothing more than a pawn? If I hadn't agreed to the engagement, Alessandra's grandfather would have merely shuffled her onto someone else. Someone that might not have been as considerate of her . . . illness."

When he put it *that* way . . .

"Then you should have at least told me the truth," she tossed over her shoulder.

"Yes," he agreed, much to her surprise. "I should have. But I kept it out of respect for Alessandra's privacy. On the eve of what was meant to be our wedding, I came to the conclusion that she wasn't well enough for marriage. That she wouldn't ever be well enough. Thus, I made the decision to take her to Kilmister Park. Her grandfather, Mountbatten, was furious. As was my grandfather. But so long as I did not break the betrothal contract, there was nothing they could do. She remained my sole responsibility until . . ." His breath expelled on a harsh sigh. "Until her death."

"She loved you," Kitty said in a whisper. Now she did pivot to look at him. In the dark, William's face was drawn. His jaw was clenched and his gaze somber. And even though she was angry at him—furious, even—how her heart ached at the same time. "She loved you, William."

I loved you, William.

"For most of my visits, Alessandra didn't even remember my name. After I ensured that she was properly cared for at Kilmister Park, and that it was the best place for her, I traveled abroad. My grandfather's disapproval was . . . expansive." His mouth twisted in a wry, humorless smile. "It took an ocean to escape it. When I finally came home, I had no intention of pursuing a courtship with *anyone*. I went to the Haversham Ball on a whim. An old friend was attending, and I hadn't spoken to him since we were at boarding school and he went off to fight the French. After he was done regaling me with his battle stories, I turned around, ready to retire for the evening . . . but there you were."

"There I was," she repeated softly.

And she remembered it.

She remembered it like it was yesterday.

"Lord William Colborne, Earl of Radcliffe, at your service, my lady."

"Lady Katherine Holden."

"A pleasure."

"I can assure you the pleasure is mine. How is it we've not yet met, Lord Radcliffe? I've attended every ball this Season, and this is the first time I've seen you."

"I was traveling abroad until recently. A business venture with a partner in Boston."

"And what, pray tell, was the manner of your business?"

"Dance with me. Dance with me, and I'll tell you."

He'd been evading her questions, she realized with a heavy thud in the pit of her stomach, from the very beginning. Distracting her with half-truths and kisses. There were a dozen instances, including the Haversham Ball, where he could have told her about Alessandra. Where he could have told her the *whole* truth as it was. And maybe she would have understood. Likely, she would have wanted him anyway. Or maybe not. But at least it would have been *her* decision. She'd have had the opportunity of choice instead of blindly falling for a man who was still entangled with another woman.

A thought struck then, insidious and loathsome. This time, she didn't want the answer.

But she had to know.

"Would you have ever married me?" The pit in her belly grew deeper as she forced herself to meet his gaze. "With Alessandra at Kilmister Park, and your engagement not officially ended, would you have asked for my hand, William?"

Brackets of tension framed his mouth. "It was a . . . delicate situation. I wouldn't have endangered Alessandra's safety. But I'd have found a way, Kitty. Our courtship was genuine."

"Our courtship was nothing but lies!" Her shout frightened a pair of nesting thrushes from the shrubbery. They took to the air, their wings beating loudly. But the flutter of feathers paled in comparison to the dull roaring in her head. "You've been lying to me from the start. Hiding things. Giving me half-truths when it suited you. Complete omissions when it didn't. How can I ever trust you again?"

Conveniently, Kitty left out her *own* lies.

What had happened to her mother.

The true state of her financial affairs.

The monster disguised as her father.

All cleverly spun lies to uphold the illusion of a perfect lady, a perfect life, a perfect potential *wife*.

A wife that William had never intended to make his own.

"If I kept things from you, it was not done out of maliciousness. I had to protect Alessandra."

"Then you shouldn't have kissed me!"

His eyes flashed in the darkness. It was her only warning before he snatched her into his arms, fingers diving into her carefully coiled coiffure whilst his other arm curved around the small of her back to pull her taut against his hard, familiar heat. "No, I shouldn't have," he agreed, his voice a grim, devilish whisper along the line of her jaw. "But I did. And I'm going to do it again."

She tried to keep her lips pressed together.

Truly, she did.

Except being kissed by William wasn't merely an assault on her mouth, it was an assault on her entire body, her heart, her very soul. Desire had never been their problem. It was what came *after* the desire that crumbled. But as her lips parted and his tongue thrust inside, she wasn't thinking about after. She wasn't even thinking about the next minute. Her thoughts, her mind, her every nerve was consumed by *now*, by William, the man she loathed to love.

Caught in a fever, she clutched the lapels of his coat, just like she had all those months ago on the terrace, and kissed him back.

Passionately.

Desperately.

Recklessly.

Anyone could have walked down the steps and seen them, giving new flame to old gossip. But the fire that swept through the rosebushes and streaked across their skin didn't singe, it *ignited*. Every feeling Kitty had been suppressing was suddenly ablaze, every tendril of longing she had ignored, every dark wish she had wanted to come true.

Because as much as she'd told herself that she didn't care if William returned, that he meant nothing to her, that he'd *lied* to her, each time she'd danced with another man, she had wished that it was William's hands that were holding her. William's eyes that were gazing at her. William's mouth that was hovering a few inches above her own.

Now it *was* him. He was here in the flesh. And while he'd lied to her, she couldn't lie to herself. She wanted him. She had always wanted him. She *would* always want him. The rest . . . the rest were merely details.

He skimmed his tongue along her bottom lip before drawing it between his teeth to suckle, the heady pressure eliciting a moan from the depths of her throat. "Katherine," he growled, the source of her ardor jutting unapologetically against her belly. "*Katherine.*"

A half stone wall designated the beginning of a walking path that invited visitors to explore deeper into the garden. Smooth river rock bit into her backside as William pushed her against it, angling his body so that she was shielded from view of the estate. If anyone happened to glance out the windows or step onto a balcony, they'd see a man they assumed was relieving himself of weak champagne. Or—more scandalously—pleasuring himself in the moonlight. What they wouldn't see was Katherine.

They wouldn't see her nails digging into William's chest when his hand went under her skirts.

Or the little line that furrowed her brow at the first stroke along her damp seam.

Certainly not the way her head lolled onto her shoulder as his finger entered her.

And they definitely wouldn't hear the mewling whimper she made when he slid in a second.

Three fluctuations of his wrist. Three, and she was already on the brink. Four, and she went soaring past it, her hot, velvet heat clenching around him as pleasure poured into her veins.

He held her upright while her knees trembled in the aftermath, pinning her between the wall and his chest. Limp, drained, dazed, she let her cheek fall over his heart. Listened to the steady *thump, thump, thump* while she slowly regained her footing. Watched the haze of clouds clear overhead, revealing a sky rich in twinkling stars. Smelled the roses, floral and sweet.

"Marry me, Kitty."

Her senses abandoned her, fleeing into the shadows as shock drained her countenance of all expression. Since the Haversham Ball, she had envisioned William speaking those words a hundred different times. A *thousand* different times. With jewels dripping from his fingers. With flowers in his hands. With a quartet of violinists behind him. But when she glanced at his hand, there was no ring there. Just the slippery glint of her own wetness. The only flowers to be found were the climbing roses that someone else had planted. And the ballroom quartet must have taken a respite, because the only sounds were the low hum of voices from within the manor and the uneven rasp of her own breath.

"What?" she said stupidly.

He traced his thumb over the arch of her cheekbone. "Marry me."

It was what wishes were made of, what *her* wishes were made of—marrying a wealthy, handsome, titled earl.

But she hadn't wished for the earl to abandon her for a year, come back, put his fingers inside her, and then propose marriage without thought, foresight, or planning. He didn't even have a ring. Or a sweeping soliloquy comparing her hair to a summer's day.

It doesn't matter, a familiar voice argued. *This is what you want, what you've always wanted.*

Yes, it was.

It was what she'd always wanted.

Yet somehow, it felt hollow. As if she'd bitten into a shiny red apple to find it empty in the middle. Not rotten. Not tart. Just . . . empty. And while she had wanted the apple, had craved the apple, had plotted to get the apple, how could she survive on its peel alone?

"You should leave." She lifted her head. "Before someone sees you."

Confusion flickered, then was quickly concealed. "Did you hear what I said?"

"I am not deaf, William. Nor am I a poor orphan child in need of your pity." She ducked under his arm and shook out her skirts in one smooth motion. "Take your marriage proposal and give it to someone who wants it, because I—I do not." The lie threatened to twist her tongue in a knot but she plowed determinedly ahead, refusing to give William the satisfaction of a stutter. Or to show just how much his unexpected return had affected her. "I'm glad you've returned safely to London. I'm sure you'll make some simpering debutante very happy."

His eyes narrowed. "Kitty—"

"No," she cut in, fully aware of just how sharp a precipice her resolve was teetering on. A single touch or a searing glance and she'd tumble right off the edge into his arms. "My answer to your incredibly romantic proposal is *no*."

Visibly frustrated, he raked a hand through his hair, shoving inky tendrils off a countenance comprised of conflicting emotions. Hurt. Anger. Bewilderment. Then a wall dropped, and she couldn't read him at all. "Fine. If that's what you want."

No, what she *wanted* was for him to give her more than two words.

I love you, Kitty. Marry me.

There, six words in total. Was that so difficult?

Mara loved her because they were sisters. Her father's love was twisted beyond recognition. Her mother couldn't love her from the grave.

So she needed someone to love her because they *chose* to. She needed someone to love her because a lot of the time, she didn't love herself. And on those dark, cloudy days, there had to be another person to carry the weight when it was too heavy a burden for her to carry alone.

A title, riches, grand houses . . . they would be nice. But they wouldn't be enough. And after everything she had endured, she wanted—she had earned—enough.

But not more than. She wasn't demanding a prince, or a king, or even a duke. Merely a wealthy earl capable of professing his love to her, and what was wrong with wanting that? What was wrong with refusing to settle for less than *that*?

Nothing, she told herself.

There was nothing wrong with it.

And she kept telling herself that as she watched her earl walk away.

Chapter Eleven

September 1812
32b Canary Street
London, England

WOMEN, WILLIAM MUSED as his carriage made a wide left-hand turn onto Canary Street, were vexing creatures. Obstinate. Willful. Argumentative. Or maybe that was just Kitty. But if she was all those things, what did it make *him* if he was preparing to knock on her door in the middle of the night and ask—nay, demand—that she marry him?

For a year, he'd dreamt of her. For a year, he'd yearned for her. For a fucking year, he'd sated his urges with his own hand rather than seek the bed of a woman who wasn't her. For a year, he'd tried to forget her.

Obviously, it hadn't worked.

While he was in Boston touring factories and attending meetings, she was all he'd thought about. When he'd hit his pillow at the end of a long day and willed himself into oblivion, she'd stolen into his mind like a wisp in the wind.

The scent of her.

The sight.

The taste.

When he couldn't take it anymore, he came home to London, to Hill House, to Kitty, the woman who had told him all those months ago that she never wanted to see him again.

Even then, knowing she was just city blocks away, he'd bid himself wait. He needed to be patient, to form a plan, as he did with his mergers. Overtaking a company without a preliminary tally of expenses or forming a detailed outline of all the players involved was rash and reckless and rarely ended well. But when the invitation to a ball had been left neatly on the corner of his desk with the rest of his correspondence, he'd known that was where Kitty would be. And he knew where he needed to go.

No.

How that word had sliced through him, straight through muscle and sinew to strike bone.

My answer to your incredibly romantic proposal is no.

Admittedly, the proposal *could* have been better. He wasn't a man accustomed to acting on impulse, yet whenever he was with Kitty, that was all he seemed to do. She was impulse, and instinct, and insatiable desire. He couldn't live without her. He'd tried and failed miserably. He *had* to have her. Beside him. In front of him. Underneath him.

"Stay here," he instructed his driver as he climbed down from the carriage. A light rain had fallen as the guests had departed the ball, and his boots splashed through shallow puddles as he made his way to Kitty's front door and raised his hand to knock.

It was half past one in the morning. Far too late—or early—for house calls. But for once, William didn't care about the damned rules of decorum. Or what his grandfather thought. Or what the *right* thing to do was.

Hang morality—he wanted Kitty. Nothing else mattered.

But before his knuckles fell upon the door with its peeling paint and rusty hinges, prepared to rouse whoever he needed to in order to gain an audience with Lady Katherine Holden, he heard a noise from within. A heavy scraping, like furniture being dragged across the floor. Brows gathering, he pressed his ear to the door... and slammed it open with his shoulder when he heard a high-pitched, feminine scream.

Kitty's scream.

Inside the house it was dark save a lone wall sconce mounted to the chimney breast. He scanned the hall and the front parlor, his gaze moving alertly through the shadows, before another scream and the sound of breaking glass had him surging up the staircase, taking the steps two at a time. At the top he was met with a long hallway, the floors stripped bare of carpet. The walls were empty as well, the paper faded around large rectangles where paintings had once hung. He registered these surroundings in the back of his mind as he followed the lingering sounds of the scream to the right and turned the corner to a rage-inducing sight.

Kitty, in her nightdress, clinging by her fingernails to a doorframe while her father tried to wrestle her out into the hall, his meaty hands clamped around her slender waist. Her hair had been pulled from its pins and there was a scratch on her cheek, a crimson streak of violence that immediately brought William's blood to boiling.

"Lord Holden, release your daughter at once," he commanded, his voice little more than a guttural snarl. Both Kitty and Eriam swung their heads to look at him. Kitty's eyes were shiny with fear. Her father's were glazed with drink and a streak of lust that turned William's stomach.

"Go away," Eriam slurred. "This doesn't concern you."

"William?" Kitty's eyes widened with recognition. "What—what are you doing here?"

"Quiet, girl!" Eriam grabbed a handful of hair and yanked.

Kitty cried out.

William charged.

He hit Eriam in the barrel of his chest, separating him from Kitty and taking him to the floor. It was like tackling a lumpy bag of potatoes, if the potatoes were filled with gin and spite. Grunting when a wildly thrown punch caught him in the stomach, he threw himself on top of Eriam and attempted to hold him down, but Kitty's father was shockingly strong for his age and inebriated state. On a howl that sounded more like a wounded dog than a man, Eriam kicked free and staggered to his feet. Hunching forward, he swiped a hand across his lips. When his fingers came away bloody, he raised indignant eyes to William.

"You cannot assault a man in his own home!" he shouted.

"And what of assaulting your own daughter?" William looked at Kitty to ensure that she was all right . . . and the quiet resignation in her beautiful blue eyes stole the very breath from his lungs and turned the edges of his vision red. "You bastard," he said hoarsely, his attention shifting back to Eriam. "You've hurt her before, haven't you? How many times? *How many fucking times?*"

Eriam's chins wobbled as he lifted them in defiance. "A child needs to respect her father. Katherine has always been too willful—"

The red blurred when William lunged and grabbed Eriam by the lapels of his jacket. He slammed the heavyset man into the wall with such brute force that, had there been paintings, they surely would have fallen.

"William!" As if from a great distance, Kitty's alarmed voice broke through the haze of scarlet. "William, what are you doing?"

Killing your father, was the first rational response his mind summoned. He managed—barely—not to say it aloud. Bringing his face within an inch of Eriam's mottled countenance, he spoke through clenched teeth as he willed his hands not to close around Eriam's thick throat and squeeze until the bastard's eyes rolled back inside his head. "You will never lay a single finger on her again. Or I'll snap it, along with your damned neck. Do you understand?"

"L-listen here," said Eriam, wheezing audibly. "You cannot tell me how to—to discipline my daughter. I'll do as I see fit—"

He did squeeze.

Just a little.

And felt a dark surge of satisfaction when Eriam began to

sputter and writhe, like a fish dangling on the sharp point of a hook.

"Perhaps I did not make myself clear," he said silkily. "That was not a question."

"Very—very well," Eriam gurgled as his face began to turn purple. "I—I understand. I understand!"

"Excellent." William released his grip and Kitty's father sagged to the ground in a crumpled heap of stale sweat. "Then we've nothing else to discuss." He rubbed his hands on his trousers, instinctively seeking to rid himself of any greasy remnants of Eriam Holden, and then held his hand out to Kitty, who had remained frozen in the doorway for the entirety of the exchange. "Let's leave."

"And go where?" she said, her arm shaking ever so slightly as she threaded her fingers through his and stepped over her father without a second glance.

Anywhere but here, in this bloody house of horrors, he thought silently. How long had Eriam stalked his own daughter? Weeks? Months? Years?

He'd seen the bruises on Kitty's wrists before. Her arms. Once, even her neck. Small, peppered marks of black and blue that she had always laughingly dismissed with a story of clumsiness or a tumble off her horse. Except on the times they'd ridden together, she'd displayed exceptional skill and ease. And there wasn't a more graceful creature on the earth than Katherine Holden. Yet he had accepted her excuses, because why would he doubt her? If she were hurt, if she were *being* hurt, then surely she would tell him. Surely she would confide in him. Surely she would ask him to help her.

But it appeared they'd both been keeping secrets.

"Home," he said, tucking her in protectively against his side, his chin cradling the top of her head as he walked her slowly, carefully to the stairs. "I'm taking you home, Kitty."

"It's the middle of the night. Your servants—"

"Won't say a word." A muscle ticked in his jaw as he struggled to calm the turbulent storm raging within. A storm of rage, of anguish and self-loathing. And under it all, under the frothy layers of complicated emotions, a sea of calm. Of hope. Of love.

"Kitty, there is something I want to—"

"Watch out!" she gasped, looking behind him.

He spun, shielding Kitty with his body as Eriam came barreling out of the shadows. Instinct drove him to drop his shoulder. It struck Eriam in the side, throwing him off balance. For an instant, he teetered. For an instant, William saw the whites of his eyes as they rolled wildly in his skull. Then he fell, crashing through the thin wooden balusters to the foyer below. He landed face down, his neck bent at an unnatural angle. Blood pooled slowly in a circle around his head. A twitch of his legs, a wet gurgling exhale, and Eriam Holden moved no more.

"William," Kitty whispered, raising her stunned gaze to his. "What have you done?"

I killed a man, was the first thought that came to mind. Followed by a resounding, *fuck*. The guilt—mountains of it—would come later, after the feverish rush in his veins had subsided. But in that moment, in that dark, dingy, dust-filled house, his only concern was for Kitty, not the damnation of his immortal soul.

"It was an accident," he said, more to himself than to her. "The body will need to be moved. If he's found like this, there will be too many questions. It was an act of self-defense. No charges will be brought. But still, there will be questions." Questions and whispers and rumors he was loath to subject himself to—to subject *Kitty* to—after what had happened with Alessandra. "Where is his bedchamber?"

Her eyes trained on the still body of her father, Kitty was slow to respond. "Down the hall, three doors on the left. Why . . . why?" What color there was in her countenance drained away when she met his gaze and saw the grim determination there. "William—"

"Go to your room and shut the door, Kitty."

"But—"

"*Shut the Goddamned door.*" He softened when she flinched. Cursed himself when he reached for her hand and she drew it away. He was handling this poorly, but bloody hell, what practice did he have in killing the father of the woman he loved and then dragging the body back up the stairs? "I'm sorry. This wasn't . . . this wasn't what I intended to happen when I came here tonight."

"Why *did* you come here?"

"For you, Katherine." This time he held onto her fingers even when she tried to pull back. "I came here for you, and when this is done, I'll be leaving with you." *And then I'll never leave you again,* he swore.

Shimmering pools of blue rose beneath a sweep of tawny lashes. "My father is dead."

"Yes," he said quietly.

A heartbeat of silence.

A quick jerk of her finger across her cheek to catch a single falling tear.

A staggered inhale of breath.

"Good riddance." She retreated into her room without another word spoken, leaving William to do what needed to be done.

Dawn was stealing in through the window in splashes of yellow and pink by the time he had finished getting Eriam into his bed, gone through the brutal process of straightening his neck, mopping up the blood, and placing an empty bottle of gin within arm's reach.

When he went to fetch Kitty, she was curled in a ball, fast asleep. He lifted her effortlessly, cradling her head on his shoulder as he brought her to his carriage that had waited through the long night and keeping it there all the way to Hill House.

A trio of maids ushered Kitty upstairs to be bathed and changed while he went to his study to send off a missive to the Archbishop of Canterbury requesting permission for a special license to marry. Such petitions were expensive and rarely granted, but money was no object and Charles Manners-Sutton was an old family acquaintance. A reply was received from Lambeth Castle before afternoon tea, and then the only thing left to do was ask Kitty to marry him.

Less than twelve hours after he'd murdered her father.

⟫⟩⟨⟪

"How are you feeling?" William's quiet question roused Kitty from where she'd been dozing on a splendidly comfortable chair in the parlor, her face turned to the golden rays of autumn light streaming in through a partially opened window.

She blinked at him, a smile already hovering in the corners of her mouth at the sight of a roguish curl dangling from his temple. A smile that fell abruptly away when her mind sharpened and her recent memories came flooding back.

The ball.

The garden.

The kiss.

The creak of footsteps in the hall.

Her father.

His hands.

William.

"You . . ." Her throat constricted as her fingers caught in the skirt of her borrowed dress, carelessly wrinkling the expensive silk. "My father . . ."

"I know." William sat heavily in the matching chair across from her own. Once they were eye level, she saw the dark, bruise-like half circles atop his cheeks and the slivers of red in the whites of his eyes. The poor man looked exhausted. "Katherine, I'm sorry. I did not mean—"

"Stop." She held up her hand, as much to halt his words as to stop herself from mutilating her gown, as it really *was* lovely silk and who knew when she would wear another of its caliber? Who knew what would happen to her now that her father was dead?

The man had done her no favors, large or small, but his presence had permitted her to remain in London during the Season. With his death, she'd be required to go into full mourning. How was she to find a husband wearing a shroud of black and abstaining from any and all social events? If she was truly sorry about anything, it was that. If William had taken anything from her, it was *that*: time.

By killing her father, he'd stolen time from her.

With his unexpected return to England and their subsequent kiss, she'd already decided that her best course of action was to find a replacement for him immediately. She could no longer afford to slowly mull her way through a dozen suitors. Not when her heart was in danger of tripping over William whenever she turned around.

Did she deserve true love?

Yes.

Was she courageous enough to pursue it?

Perhaps not.

She'd loved William, and look where that had gotten her. Look *what* that had gotten her: twelve months' worth of misery and missing him. Now he was back, her father was dead, and she would have to remove herself from the marriage mart or risk ruining her reputation and any chance she had of making a favorable match.

"Will my father's demise arouse any suspicion?" she asked bluntly.

William gave a curt shake of his head. "No, but you and the Duchess of Southwick will have to make funeral arrangements. I can help—"

"Heaven knows Mara needs something to do." Belatedly, Kitty considered her sister's feelings and felt her first true twinge of remorse. Not for Eriam—good riddance to him, as she'd told William—but for the pain his death would undoubtedly cause her more emotionally sensitive sibling. Mara had wanted to believe their father had become better, and she'd let her believe it because it was either that or risk being dragged away to Southwick Castle to live under Mara's hovering thumb. She wouldn't burden her sister with the truth—that Eriam had only gotten worse—which meant Mara would don her mourning clothes with a genuine sense of mourning.

Or perhaps not. Perhaps some sins were too big to be forgiven. Perhaps some secrets were too big to be forgotten.

"He killed her," she said, feeling the piercing burn of William's stare as she lowered her gaze to her lap. "I've never told anyone that before. Mara and I don't speak of it. I shouldn't be speaking of it now, but . . . well, what does it matter?" A bitter smile twisted her lips. "He pushed her down the same stairs that claimed his own life. Poetic justice, I suppose. Mara saw it all. I was hiding under a blanket. I don't remember how old I was. Nine, maybe. Or ten. Ten sounds right. I don't think he did it on purpose, but he still did it, so it counts the same, wouldn't you say?"

"Katherine . . ." William's voice, raw and ragged, caused her chin to lift and their eyes to meet. "Are you telling me that your father murdered your mother?"

"Yes," she said simply, and her hackles rose at the flicker of pity that she saw in the depths of his obsidian gaze. "Don't look at me like that," she snapped, leaping up from her chair to stab a finger at him. "This is precisely why I never told you. Why Mara and I vowed to never tell anyone. Because of that look. The one on your face. The look that would follow us around for the rest of our lives if people knew the truth."

William's countenance went blank as he straightened in his seat. "Last night, when I arrived and your father was hurting you . . . that wasn't the first time."

Kitty pursed her lips. She didn't want to be trapped in this conversation, but she was the one who had opened the door. Now she had no choice but to walk through it into a room that she'd spent her entire life guarding. "No."

"How many times has he put his hands on you before?"

"I've no idea." She gave a negligent shrug. "I lost count a long while ago."

It wasn't pity that flashed in William's eyes when he surged forward, closed the space between them in a single step, and grabbed her by the arms, fingers wrapping painlessly around her flesh to yank her against him. It was pure, unadulterated fury. "You should have told me," he growled.

"As you told me about Alessandra?" she countered, ignoring the leap in her belly that always came from being this close to him.

"That's different."

"A secret is a secret, William."

"I could have protected you."

Instead, you left me.

She didn't say the words out loud, but they were there nevertheless, swirling around in the chasm of hurt they'd both been digging since the night they'd met each other. Lies stacked on lies. Secrets stacked on secrets. And under it all, a passion that they'd never been able to control.

"I could have protected you," he repeated, so quietly that she wondered if he was speaking to her . . . or himself. "I'm sorry, Kitty. I'm sorry that I wasn't there."

"It's over," she said, striving for a flippant tone that fell flat upon delivery. "What is done is done, and I for one am glad—"

"Marry me," he interrupted, his palm cupping her cheek. "I want you to marry me. I want you to be my wife. I want to make sure that I am there when you need me."

She expelled her breath on a frustrated hiss. "It's not that *simple*, William."

"Why not?"

"Because . . ." But for once, she didn't have an answer. There was no barbed quip on the tip of her tongue. No ready defense. No argument. Given the events of the past twelve hours, why *shouldn't* she marry William? In the midst of a storm, a ship would be foolish to turn away from the nearest port in hopes that a better haven might be around the next bend.

Maybe she was wrong, Kitty reasoned. Maybe... maybe marriage was the one thing that would fix everything.

After all, how much worse could things get?

"Very well," she said, leaning into the weight of his hand. "I'll marry you."

CHAPTER TWELVE

May 1813

"O I!" JACK'S BELLOWING voice carried up the stairs at Hill House, rousing Kitty from her restless slumber.

After her and William's fraught discussion in his bed following their lovemaking, she'd had trouble sleeping. For five nights she had tossed and turned while pretending everything was fine in the light of day. Much longer and she'd no longer be able to disguise the shadows under her eyes. *Something* had to be done. She just didn't know what that something was.

"There's a man 'ere!" Jack went on. "Says he wants to speak to the Marquess of Kentwood. Whoever the bloody 'ell that is. I told him we ain't got no marquess 'ere, but he won't listen."

Where, Kitty thought crossly as she dragged a pillow across her face and gave serious consideration to smothering herself with it, *were the damned servants?*

As a countess, sleeping in past the ten o'clock hour was a luxury afforded her by the various maids, footmen, housekeeper, and butler that kept the household running like clockwork. At last count, Hill House had a full staff of eighteen, while Radcliffe Park employed over fifty. Why, then, couldn't one of *them* deal with Jack's carrying on at—she lowered the pillow to glare at the mahogany longcase clock in the corner of her bedchamber—half past seven in the morning?

"KITTY! ARE YE AWAKE? THERE'S A MAN 'ERE—"

"I heard you the first time!" she shouted, throwing the pillow onto the floor and following it with her feet. Grabbing the blue silk wrapper hanging from her bedpost, she knotted it around her waist before stomping into the hallway where she passed a scullery maid carrying a basket of linens.

"Have you seen Mr. Davies?" she asked, referring the butler. "Or Mrs. Wilson?" The housekeeper. "Or Stevens?" Her husband's valet, dreadful man that he was, should at least have been somewhere about. She would have asked for *her* personal attendant, Elizabeth, but the poor girl had been under the weather for the past three days and Kitty didn't want to wake her if she was resting.

"I—I believe they're in a meeting, my lady."

"Meeting?" said Kitty, mystified. "What meeting?"

"On the first Monday of every month, Mr. Davies gathers all the staff to discuss our duties, my lady. We meet in the summer kitchen behind the manor, so as not to disturb you or Lord Radcliffe." The maid hesitated. "Should I fetch Mr. Davies for you, my lady? Or is there something I can help you with? You're up unusually early."

"I'm aware." Kitty leaned a hip against the wall. "Don't you hear the yelling?"

"Do you mean Miss Jack, my lady?"

"Yes, I mean *Miss* Jack."

"Mr. Stevens has instructed us to . . . ah . . ."

"Go on," she said when the maid paused, her cheeks filling with color. "What has the delightful Mr. Stevens instructed you to do?"

"Ignore her, my lady."

Kitty's eyes narrowed. "Oh he has, has he?"

"Yes, my lady. He was quite insistent."

"I see. And my husband?"

"Lord Radcliffe left, my lady. Nearly an hour ago. A sunrise ride in the park, I believe."

"Thank you . . . I'm afraid I don't know your name."

"Emily, my lady."

"Thank you, Emily. I'll see to Jack." *And then to Stevens*, Kitty added silently as she continued on down the stairs to where Jack was standing in the middle of the front hall, dressed in her borrowed brown trousers and white linen shirt with her red hair stuffed under the floppy hat she'd insisted on buying to replace her old one.

"Where are the clothes I bought you?" Kitty sighed, crossing her arms.

"They make me sneeze."

"Clothes cannot make you *sneeze*. Especially when they're woven of the finest fabric money can buy." Clothes that Kitty would have sold her left arm for when *she* was Jack's age. Lifting a ratty curl poking out from her young charge's hat, she sighed again. "You're a girl, Jacqueline. You cannot continue to parade about in boys' attire. It's unseemly."

"Can't run in a dress. Or skip. Or climb through an empty window to pinch a piece of silver."

"Young ladies do not run, or skip, or *steal*."

"Being a young lady is boring. I'd rather act like a boy."

"While you're living under my roof, you'll act like a girl." She tugged on Jack's curl before releasing it. "A girl who wears dresses and chews food with her mouth closed and doesn't wake the entire household by screaming nonsense before morning tea has been prepared."

"Wasn't nonsense," Jack said with a belligerent jerk of her chin. "And maybe I don't want to live under your roof anymore. Maybe I want to go back to where I was living."

Kitty arched a brow even as a chord of panic ran through her at the idea of Jack leaving. As loud and disruptive as the little hellion may have been, she couldn't imagine living without her. What had begun as an uncharacteristic act of charity had turned into so much more. Jack wasn't just an orphan. She was... she was turning into family. And she couldn't leave. Kitty wouldn't allow it.

"There will be no divorce. You won't leave me."

Unbidden, William's words rose to mind and she pushed them away. It wasn't the same. Her keeping Jack here and William keeping her in their marriage were two different things. She wanted Jack to remain because she cared for her and wanted to keep her safe, while William...

"I care for you, Kitty. Deeply."

It was different, she told herself.

Completely different.

"You want to live on the streets?" she snapped, returning her attention to Jack. "With the stench of summer soon to arrive? I think not. In a few weeks' time we'll be packing our trunks and leaving London for the countryside where you can practice your ambitious climbing skills on a tree, so long as you're wearing a dress. Until then, I'll ask you to keep your voice to a dull roar until *after* luncheon and if you're bored, you can practice your embroidery. There's no need to invent visitors for attention."

Jack's face wrinkled as if she'd just bitten into a lemon. "I hate embroidery. Jabbed a needle clear through my thumb the last time you made me try it. Bled like a stuck pig. And I wasn't inventing nothin'. There *is* a man here. He was poundin' at the door and no one was around to let him in, so I did. Seemed all important like. Was carryin' a bunch of papers and said he had to speak to the Marquess of Ken... Ken... I don't remember the bloody name."

"Don't curse, and it is Kentwood," Kitty said automatically, her mind beginning to spin. "He's seeking Lord Kentwood, but I don't know why he thinks he'd find him here."

She could count on one hand the number of encounters she'd had with William's father. The Marquess and Marchioness of Kentwood had been at her wedding, of course, along with William's grandfather, the Duke of Cumberland. She'd also enjoyed—tolerated might be a better word—Lady Kentwood's attentions before she and William were married. But since then, William's family had been conspicuously absent from their lives . . . and any time she'd attempted to broach the subject, he'd quickly turned to a different topic of conversation.

Given that estranged in-laws weren't the *worst* thing in the world, she'd never gotten to the bottom of why William kept such a distance from his parents and grandfather. After all, she knew better than most what a burden family could be. But she was quite curious what would bring a stranger here at such an unfashionable hour, and why he would request an audience with the Marquess of Kentwood instead of the Earl of Radcliffe.

"Where did you put him?" she asked Jack.

"In there." Jack jabbed a thumb over her shoulder in the direction of the receiving parlor, a room directly off the foyer tastefully decorated in shades of blue.

"Don't let him leave. I'll be right back." Dashing up the stairs to her bedchamber, Kitty once again passed Emily in the hallway and this time beckoned for the maid to follow her. "I need to dress," she said, already untying her wrapper. "Quickly."

In a matter of minutes—no small feat—she had changed from her night clothes into a yellow frock with capped sleeves and a burgundy sash that fit snugly beneath the natural curve of her bosom. Pearls at her ears matched the pearl comb that Emily expertly affixed to her blonde curls, sweeping them up into a wispy chignon that accentuated the defining arch of Kitty's cheekbones.

"You're quite good at this," she complimented the maid, and Emily blushed in response.

"Thank you, my lady," she said shyly, averting her gaze from the oval mirror where Kitty was openly admiring her reflection. "You're too kind."

"And *you* are now my second lady's maid."

Emily's mouth dropped open. In the hierarchy of the serving staff, a scullery maid—her prior position—was as far removed from a lady's maid as a footman was from a butler, and such a promotion was practically unheard of. "Oh, no, my lady, I couldn't—"

"It's already done." Back down the stairs Kitty went, through the foyer, and breathlessly into the parlor where she found a man waiting for her, holding a clutch of papers to his chest just as Jack had described. But she'd failed to mention the man's dour expression or the moustache that ran across his top lip like a long, scraggly caterpillar.

"Hello," she said pleasantly, nudging the door closed behind her with a discreet push of her heel. "How can I help you, Mister . . . ?"

"Thomas Greer." Mr. Greer had pale-gray eyes that darted around the room before landing on Kitty. The caterpillar gave a vague twitch. "I am a solicitor charged with a very specific task this morning. I should like to speak with Lord Kentwood at once. It is a most urgent matter."

"I am afraid your urgency is misplaced, Mr. Greer, as Lord Kentwood is not here. Should you like to speak with his son—"

"Son?" the solicitor interrupted. The caterpillar wiggled in annoyance. "I was not aware Lord Kentwood had yet produced a male heir. I shall have to update the entail at once."

Something strange was going on.

Pouring herself a glass of lemonade from a pitcher sitting beside a vase filled with freshly picked daffodils, Kitty took a measured sip as she studied Mr. Greer over the rim of her glass. "I confess to being somewhat bemused, sir. Why is it you wish an audience with Lord Kentwood?"

"That is a private matter best discussed with the marquess."

Kitty decided to change tactics. "Lemonade?" she said sweetly, pouring a second glass and holding it out. "It's a tad sweet for my personal taste, but you know what they say about sugar and honey. And do have a seat. My husband should be returning from his morning ride soon. Once he arrives, I'm sure we can sort this matter out."

The caterpillar jerked in surprise. "Lord Kentwood doesn't know, does he? Or you, for that matter. I had assumed a family member would have reached out, or at the very least sent a note, but perhaps . . ."

"Lord Kentwood doesn't know *what?*" she said with growing exasperation. "Mr. Greer, my husband—"

"With all due condolences, my lady, Lord Kentwood *is* now your husband. Pending a petition to the Crown to claim the title, naturally. His father passed from this world early yesterday morning. Peacefully in his sleep, by all accounts. I've been sent by the Duke of Cumberland to ensure that his new heir's affairs are all in order, and that Lord Kentwood makes his petition with all haste. His Grace should like a smooth transition."

Kitty nearly dropped her glass. Lemonade sloshed over the top as she set it hastily aside on the nearest table and stared at Mr. Greer with her mouth agape, not bothering to disguise her shock. "My father-in-law is . . . dead?" *And I am now a marchioness.*

Once, such a thought would have filled her with giddy elation. Given the current state of her marriage, however, it did nothing more than place a sour taste on the back of her tongue. Divorcing an earl, while remarkably difficult, wouldn't have been *completely* impossible. But there was no way Parliament would act to permit her to legally separate herself from the direct heir of a dukedom. As a marchioness, her duty was clear: produce a male child and continue the proper succession of one of the country's oldest, most prestigious family lines. A line already fraught with tension and tragedy. A line that wouldn't look the other way if she disavowed herself of her marriage.

In truth, Kitty acknowledged with a sinking feeling, this was *always* to have been her fate. William's father was mortal, after all, and mortal men succumbed to all sorts of maladies. She'd never imagined it would happen this soon, but it was bound to happen someday. Time granted mercy to no one.

"I am sorry for the inconvenience, Mr. Greer, but I must ask you to leave and return later this afternoon." The shock slipped from her countenance and was replaced with a cool resolve. "I should like to deliver this sad news to my husband without the presence of his grandfather's solicitor. He should be allowed to mourn before being required to sign papers."

The caterpillar twitched with disapproval even as Mr. Greer gathered his belongings and walked stiffly to the door. "I shall be at my offices. Please have Lord Kentwood send for me before the end of day."

"I shall ensure that he does."

⤞⤝

THE FUNERAL OF the late Marquess of Kentwood was a somber affair attended by some of the *ton*'s most prestigious and influential members, including a personal envoy of King George. Kitty sat at the front of the church in a hard wooden pew squished between William's mother and grandmother, both of whom wept daintily into monogrammed handkerchiefs.

While the priest droned on, she cast a quick glance at William who was seated beside his grandfather, the Duke of Cumberland, in the pew directly across from theirs. His attention was fixed on the pulpit and the elm coffin in front of it, and he gave no indication that he felt her stare aside from the flicker of a muscle high on his freshly shaven jaw. A muscle ticking in her own jaw, she turned her gaze forward.

Over the past week, while preparations were made, papers and deeds were signed (under the watchful eye of Mr. Greer), and the late marquess's body was transported to London, where he would be buried alongside his brother in the private family tomb, Kitty and William had hardly seen each other, let alone spoken.

Whilst the house had been draped in swaths of black and Kitty had exchanged her lush, colorful wardrobe for obsidian silks and ebony tulle (such a dreadful shade, it paired horribly with her complexion), William had spent most of his time either in his office or with his grandfather. Becoming the direct heir of one of the largest, most powerful dukedoms in England was no small task, but it appeared the newly minted Marquess of Kentwood had stepped into the role with the iron determination that he was renowned for.

As soon as his father was laid to rest, they were bound for Radcliffe Park, a stone's throw from Kentwood Manor, where his mother would continue to reside. As the Marquess of Kentwood *and* Earl of Radcliffe, William now owned some of the most impressive estates, houses, and hunting lodges in Great Britain, surpassed only by his grandfather and Mara's husband, the Duke of Southwick, whose sprawling countryside manor encompassed more than ten thousand acres.

Finally, Kitty had everything that she'd ever dreamed of when she was a debutante wearing hand-me-down dresses and glass jewelry: the wealth, the title, the prestige. One day, she and Mara would *both* be duchesses. A far cry from their humble beginnings as the abused daughters of a lowly viscount. Kitty should have been happy. She should have been *ecstatic*. But as she snuck a second glance at her husband, she only felt a lingering sense of despair. Yes, she might have had everything she'd ever dreamed of, but without William's love, she was still living in a nightmare.

Later, when the last of the guests had trickled from the house after expressing their condolences and Jack was snoring in her room down the hall and William was shut away in his office, Kitty sat in front of her dressing mirror brushing her hair by candlelight. The rhythmic motion of pulling the bristles through her blonde tendrils was soothing, a mindless task that allowed her to rest after a long, exhausting day of being on display. Her mouth ached from all of the smiles she'd given. And her heart . . . well, her heart ached from something else entirely.

We fuck and we fight, William had told her that night. *There's nothing in between.*

Truer words, she thought, her tired lips twisting in a wry smile as she worked the brush through a stubborn tangle. She'd given a half-hearted attempt at speaking to him tonight, but neither had been ready for the conversation they needed to have, and they'd retreated to their respective chambers after wishing each other a cordial evening.

Tomorrow, after breakfast, they would leave for Radcliffe Park, she and Jack in one carriage and William in another. Why share a barouche when they didn't share a bedroom? Once they were at their country estate, it would become even easier to lead separate lives. To be polite when they were seen together in public and then retreat to their own spaces in private. They'd spend their days apart and then have dinner together at night. If one or both of them indulged in a bit too much wine, they'd likely find themselves in a compromising position. Then she would go back to her chamber, or he would return to his, and when the sun rose all would be as it had been.

After the ground turned silver with frost and their obligatory mourning period had expired, they would return to London and make their official debut as the new Marquess and Marchioness of Kentwood. Parties and balls and charity dinners would require they spend more time together, but not much. Then the bite of winter would ease, the heat of summer would roll in, and back to the country they'd go. Maybe with a babe in her belly this time. Maybe not. And another year would pass. Then another. And another. With nothing changing and no escape from the life she had convinced herself she wanted.

"*Ouch!*" she exclaimed when she gave the brush an extra hard yank and it snagged on another tangle. Glaring at the brush as if *it* were the source of all her problems, she tossed it into a basket along with all of the other personal items she was bringing to Radcliffe Park. Combs, ribbons, pins, and silk stockings. Sliding open the drawer of her dressing table to make sure she wasn't missing anything of importance, her gaze landed on a thin book shoved toward the back, its spine covered in faded green fabric. Brow furrowing, she pulled the book from the drawer and opened it on her lap. Mara was the reader in the family, not her. If it wasn't a newspaper filled with titillating gossip or a magazine bursting with the latest fashions from Paris, then she wasn't interested. Why, then, was this book tucked away among her most personal possessions?

She flipped through the first few pages and found them blank, indicating it was intended to be a journal comprised of her innermost thoughts and feelings. One that she'd obviously never used in the past and wasn't likely to use in the future. She started to close the book when something fell from amidst the thin sheets of ivory parchment. It floated to the floor in a spiral of graceful motion and then slid, quite inconveniently, under her chair.

With a huff of breath, she took the candle from her dressing table and used the flickering yellow light to guide her eye as she got down on her hands and knees. When she saw what had fallen from the journal, her heart stilled. There, resting on the flat polished surface of an oak floorboard, was a perfectly preserved lilac bloom.

Being pressed between the pages of the journal had flattened the petals and time had stolen its color, but a hint of violet still clung to the delicate corolla. With trembling fingers, she picked up the lilac by its brittle stem and slowly pressed it to her chest. Just as she'd done when William had given it to her during their first carriage ride together two years ago.

So much had happened since then. So much heartbreak. So much miscommunication. So much hurt. And yet... and yet, some things remained the same. She and William were still together. Not as happy and blissfully hopeful as they'd been on that beautiful spring day in May, but together nevertheless. Bound by the laws of marriage and the deep well of secrets that they shared.

Unbidden, her sister's voice rang her head as she sat on the floor in a pool of flickering candlelight with the dried lilac held to her breast.

Make sure it's your husband that you're running from, Mara had told her. And she'd brushed the words off, as a younger sibling often did when it was the older speaking them. But now they resonated. Now, at last, they made sense.

She'd become so fixated with running away from William that she had never stopped to consider what might happen if she ran *toward* him. Toward the man she loved despite everything. Toward the man who made her pulse race and her skin tingle. Toward the man who frustrated her. The man who angered her. The man who had given her a lilac blossom she'd treasured enough to keep protected even during the most tumultuous of storms.

Rising from the floor, she carefully tucked the flower back between the pages of the journal and placed the journal in the basket beside the brush. Then she met her own doe-eyed gaze in the mirror above the dressing table as a smile—this one genuine—curved her lips.

She, Lady Katherine Colborne, Marchioness of Kentwood and Countess of Radcliffe, was going to do the unthinkable. Perhaps even the impossible.

She was going to court her husband.

Chapter Thirteen

William did not grieve his father's death. To grieve someone, you had to have loved them first. And while he had liked his father well enough, that aloof amicability had never extended into love. Not to say that he was *glad* his father had died. While some heirs waited for their fathers to expire with bated breath, William had never wished ill will upon his. He hadn't wished . . . anything. Except to be left alone. And while the late marquess had failed at almost all other aspects of his life—he'd been an absent father, a faithless husband, a terrible lord—he'd excelled at forgetting he had a son.

So no, William did not arrive at Radcliffe Park in the throes of grief.

But he did arrive in a temper.

"What do you mean, my wife is not here?" he growled at Stevens. A steady spring rain lashed at the windows of the front hall and water dripped onto the carpet when Stevens removed his coat. "She left London before me!"

The valet remained expressionless as he draped the wet garment over his forearm. "I am not certain, my lord. I can ask—"

"Kitty went to visit her sister." This from Jack, who entered the foyer by way of sliding down the banister. As usual, she wore boys' trousers and her feet were bare. Red coils of hair framed a mischievous grin that widened when she looked at Stevens, and the valet's countenance turned a distinctive shade of purple as she stuck out her tongue at him. "Wouldn't let me go. Said it was 'woman's business' and since I ain't got no tits yet, I had to stay here. This house is *enormous*." She spun around in a circle. "How many rooms does it have?"

Clearing his throat to disguise a snort of laughter that would have no doubt sent Stevens straight into an apoplectic fit, William strove for a tone of solemnity when he said, "Radcliffe Park has eighty-four rooms."

"Bloody 'ell! Eighty-four? I can't even count that high!"

"How shocking," Stevens sneered.

"I trust your accommodations are to your liking?" William asked, the corners of his eyes crinkling.

Jack nodded enthusiastically. "The bed is *huge*. And there's a bathtub. Right in the room!"

"Then we can expect you to bathe with more"—Stevens's nose wrinkled—"frequency?"

"Kitty told me to tell ye that she'll be back for dinner," said Jack with a withering glance at the valet so reminiscent of Katherine that William wasn't able to withhold a chuckle. While his wife's fashion sense had yet to rub off on her young charge, it was clear that Jack had picked up a few of her . . . personality traits.

"Did she say anything else?" he asked, removing his damp gloves and handing them off to Stevens before dismissing the valet with a curt nod.

"Just the usual. Don't steal anythin', don't make a nuisance of myself, and don't slide down the stairs." Jack's forehead wrinkled as she looked over her shoulder at the banister and then back at William, a rare hint of guilt in her green eyes. "Can ye not tell her I did that? I've been trying."

"Trying what?" he asked, suppressing another smile.

"To follow the rules. Ye nabobs just have so *many* of them."

"We do," he agreed before lowering his voice to a conspiratorial whisper. "But can I share a secret?"

Jack nodded cautiously.

"Sliding down banisters isn't one of them. At least not at Radcliffe Park." And because it felt right, because it felt paternal despite there being no blood shared between them, he reached out and ruffled Jack's hair. A small gesture. Meaningless to most. But it was something his own father had never done to him and if the widening of Jack's eyes were any indication, something no parent of hers had ever done either. "Well then," he said gruffly, crossing his hands behind his back. "I, ah, have business to attend to in my study."

He could feel Jack staring at him as he walked quickly away. Just as he felt the odd pang in the center of his chest where his heart resided. He closed the door to his study and then leaned against it while he waited for the tightness to ease. But to his discomfort, it didn't disappear. Rather, it warmed and began to spread, like honey being drizzled into a warm cup of tea. Vaguely, he recognized the warmth for what it was.

Love.

Not the hot, complicated love he had for Kitty. This was a milder, more comfortable version. Wrapped in protectiveness and a fatherly instinct he hadn't known he possessed. His interactions with Jack had been infrequent at best, but he'd still watched her from afar. She'd been living in his house, after all. Eating his food. Cheating in piquet. Driving his valet mad. And all the while, completely unbeknownst to him, working her way into his heart.

The irony, he acknowledged, pinching the bridge of his nose, was bittersweet. Over the years, how often had he blamed himself for his father's lack of attention, lack of love, lack of simple bloody *interest*? Henry Colborne had rarely given his son the time of day, let alone shown him anything that might be construed as affection. And in the way of the children, William had assumed the fault was his. When he became an adult, he'd tried not to think about it at all. But he had. Of course he had.

Every fight with Kitty that ended with her wanting to leave him, to leave their marriage, he'd thought *and why shouldn't she? If I am not worthy of my own father's love, how could I demand it of my wife?*

The answer was he couldn't. You couldn't make someone love you.

But you *could* make them stay, and so that's what he had done.

Over, and over, and over again he'd denied Kitty's request for divorce . . . and every time she'd asked, every time those big blue eyes had implored him to let her go, the little boy inside of him had felt the sting of rejection once more. Because if his father had taught him anything in the pitifully small amount of time they'd spent together, it was that he was unlovable. And somewhere along the way, he'd taken that to mean *he* was also incapable of loving, that he was incapable of giving what he'd never received himself. But that wasn't true, because he loved Jack. The scrawny, foul-mouthed street urchin had wormed her way into his life and under his skin. Proving that he *could* love. That he wasn't his father. That he was capable of more than the man whose blood ran in his veins. But perhaps that was the saddest realization of all—that he was able to give love . . . he just didn't deserve to receive it.

Wearily, William rose to his feet and crossed the room to his desk to pour himself a drink, his steps heavy both from the long ride that had brought him here and the weight of emotions burdening his chest. He may have loved Jack, and God knew he loved Kitty in all of the ways a woman could be loved. But that didn't mean they loved him. That *she* loved him. Why would she? How could she? And if he truly loved her . . . if he truly loved her, perhaps it was time to give her what she wanted, what she'd always wanted, if he was being completely honest with himself.

Her freedom.

"I AM SORRY again that we could not attend the funeral." Small lines of regret etched themselves across Mara's fair forehead as she joined Kitty on the veranda overlooking the rear gardens of Southwick Castle. Rain, as it had for most of the night and morning, fell in a gray drizzle while steam rose in a cozy tendril from the cup of coffee she delivered to Kitty before she sat beside her on a generously upholstered, wicker-framed sofa. "I haven't been feeling well, and feared I wouldn't be able to make the trip. Ambrose, bless him, didn't want to leave me in such a state."

Kitty drew a knee to her chest beneath the folds of her midnight-blue traveling habit and took a sip of coffee. After delivering Jack straight to Radcliffe Park, she'd instructed the driver to continue on the five or so miles to Southwick Castle for an impromptu visit with her sister. She needed advice, and as she didn't have many friends, at least none in happy marriages, that meant she needed Mara.

In a world where women married for appearance, title, money, or a combination of all three, the Duchess of Southwick was a dissenter. She *had* married her husband for love, and while the beginning of her union with Ambrose had been quite rocky, they'd since sailed off to blissfully peaceful waters filled with sunsets and rainbows and dolphins. Kitty may not have wanted the dolphins—she loathed boats and anything to do with the ocean, as stepping off shore never failed to make her stomach do an array of acrobatics—but she did want the sunsets. She wanted the rainbows. She wanted the happily-ever-after. She wanted *William*. Not the earl or the marquess—she wanted the man. The man who had broken her heart, put it together, and then broken it again. Loving William had never been easy. It would never *be* easy. They were both too stubborn and too set in their ways for that. But if she bent for anyone, she wanted it to be him. And while scars weren't pretty, they could be strong.

"The funeral was the same as any other," she said dismissively. "William's mother cried a tad more than I thought she would, particularly given that three of her husband's mistresses were in attendance. And I have to wear a dark color palette for the next six months—you *know* how black washes out my skin—but it went as well as could be expected."

"And William?" Mara asked, scooping a spoonful of sugar into her coffee. "How is he?"

"He seems to be handling his father's death well. They were not very close."

"And you?" her sister said softly. "How are you, Kitty?"

There was absolutely no reason for Mara's question to bring a rush of tears to Kitty's eyes, but it did. Maybe because she was tired and hadn't slept well the night before. Maybe because the coffee was a touch too bitter. Or maybe . . . just maybe . . . it was because Mara's concern was a reminder that no matter what happened, she had a sister who loved her. A sister who had always taken care of her. A sister who had, quite literally, shielded her from blows meant for her. A sister she had taken for granted and taken her anger out on. A sister who would still drop whatever she was doing at a moment's notice to sit with her on a veranda in the rain. Blinking the pinprick of waterworks away, Kitty cleared her throat and said, "That is why I've come here, actually. I need to know how you did it."

Mara's brow creased. "How I did what?"

"Made Ambrose fall in love with you, of course."

"Oh," her sister said with a startled laugh. "I . . . well . . . I'm not sure, to be honest. I don't know if it was any one thing, but rather a combination of little things that helped us both realize how much we meant to the other."

"He did save you from the wild dogs," Kitty reminded her. Several months ago, Mara had gone for a nighttime walk in the orchards of this very estate and had been set upon by a ruthless pack of feral canines. Had Ambrose not gone searching for her, it was likely they wouldn't be having this conversation today. While fighting the dogs off, Ambrose had sustained a bite and a subsequent infection that had nearly taken his life.

"Yes, he did." Mara shuddered. "On days like these, his leg

still pains him. When we were last in London I went to visit Dr. Chadwick and she gave me a poultice to wrap around the scar tissue. It does seem to help ease the ache. Do you know she has eight cats? I managed to count them all when I was in her office."

"Why would anyone want eight cats?"

"She's an American."

"That explains it." Kitty paused. "I was short with you, wasn't I? While you were caring for Ambrose and I came to visit, I was terribly unkind and you asked me to leave."

"Oh, Kitty, I'm sorry—"

"No," she interrupted, "*I'm* sorry, Mara. I'm sorry for how I've acted. How I've treated you. How selfish I've been. I . . . I became so accustomed to being your little sister that I forgot I was an adult, responsible for my own decisions and my own choices. I took my anger out on you . . . I've been *taking* my anger out on you . . . and I shouldn't have."

"But you were right." Her luminous brown eyes glistened with tears. "I did marry Ambrose and leave you, Kitty. With *him*." She didn't say their father's name aloud, but she didn't have to. They both knew to whom she was referring in the instinctive flinch of their bones. "I wrote to you. I asked how you were doing, and when you wrote back you insisted that you were fine. That you'd met a dashing young earl and your life was perfect, but in my heart . . . in my heart I knew better."

"You were a bride with her own problems to be solved. Your focus should not have been on me, and I shouldn't have expected it to be." When Kitty's tears threatened to return, she kept them at bay with a watery smile.

How maudlin they must have appeared, sniffling into their cups on a rainy day. A duchess and a marchioness crying over past regrets when there was far more suffering to be found in the world than what resided on a beautiful veranda. But pain was pain, and Kitty was determined to make amends for the hurt she had caused to the person who had loved her the longest.

"Before Alessandra died, William came to me. He wanted to make amends. To ask me to wait for him while he saw her settled. But he didn't know how long that would take, and I was too proud and too damned stubborn to wait. I didn't come here for the country air, Mara. And I didn't come here for you, my sister, who had just been abandoned by her husband. I came to Southwick Castle to hide. I came here to hide," she repeated softly as a single tear, so light that she hardly felt it, traced a watery trail down her cheek, "and when I returned to London for the Season, I thought I could forget William and move on. But no matter how many men I danced with, he was the only one I thought about. I saw his face everywhere. I heard his voice in my dreams. He was an ocean away and I still couldn't escape him."

"Because you loved him," Mara prodded gently. "Even after all that had happened with Alessandra, you still loved him."

"I did love him." Blast it, where were all of these tears *coming from*? "And I hated him. And I missed him. And I wanted to never see him again. Then suddenly, there he was. A year later, standing in the middle of a ballroom, just like the first night that we met."

"You realized how much you meant to each other," said Mara, picking up the story as she had been told it, "and when he proposed to you in the gardens, you said yes."

Simple, Kitty thought dimly. It sounded so simple that way. But the truth—the truth she'd kept hidden from her sister—was much more violent.

Standing up, she went to the railing and stared blindly out into the rain as a chill worked its way down her spine. "The proposal didn't happen . . . precisely like that."

"What do you mean?"

Kitty had grown up on a steady diet of secrets. Her mother's murder. Her father's abuse. The money she had pretended to have. But secrets did not sustain the soul. They destroyed it. And she was tired, so bloody tired, of starving her soul for the sake of keeping her secrets safe. Closing her eyes, she took a deep breath. Then she told Mara everything about that terrible night, leaving no detail out. And when she was finished, when she had completely purged herself of lies, she turned around slowly, bracing herself for condemnation.

Instead, she had only comfort waiting.

"Oh, *Katherine*." On a hiccupping sob, Mara rose from the sofa and wrapped her in a tight embrace that forced the air from her lungs. "You said you found Father dead from drink! I had no idea. You should have told me. I could have helped you. Supported you."

"You're not . . . you're not upset?"

"Only that you withheld the truth from me." Taking a step back, Mara adopted the stern-older-sister expression she'd perfected when they both still wore pinafores. "Father was . . . Father was deplorable, Kitty. What he did to Mother . . . what he did to me . . . what he threatened to do to you . . ." She pressed her lips together. "There was no goodness in him. Only darkness. I was relieved when you wrote me that he'd died. Knowing *how* it happened does not change that."

"William does not like to talk about it." Kitty leaned heavily against the railing. "He blames himself for our father's death and for Alessandra's suicide."

Mara frowned. "Neither was his fault. Not really."

"*I* know that, and *you* know that, but *he* doesn't know that."

"Have you told him?"

"I . . ." Her mouth opened. Closed. "I'm not sure."

Between the yelling, and the lovemaking, and the long stretches of stony silence that had consumed their marriage, had she ever actually told William that she did not hold him responsible for what had happened to her father? Had she ever told him that if she searched deep inside of herself, she—grudgingly—understood why he had done what he'd done where Alessandra was concerned?

No.

No, she didn't believe that she had.

"You should," said Mara when she shook her head. "Because I did not *make* Ambrose fall in love with me. Love is not something that can be ordered or coerced. It must bloom naturally in rich, healthy soil that can sustain it through the inevitable seasons of a marriage. Only when Ambrose was vulnerable with me and I with him, only when we trusted each other with our innermost thoughts and feelings, did our garden start to grow and blossom into the love that we have today."

Kitty rolled her eyes. "William isn't a daffodil, Mara."

"And you're certainly no buttercup," her sister quipped. "But you are deserving of loving and being loved, Kitty. No matter how hard our father worked to convince you otherwise."

"I should go back to Radcliffe Park," she said when her throat swelled yet again. Had she known that her conversation with Mara would be this emotional, she'd have brought cucumber slices with her. There was nothing worse than puffy eyes. "William will likely have arrived by now, and we . . . we have much to discuss."

"I'll be here if you need me." Mara accompanied Kitty to the entrance hall where she donned her bonnet and gloves. "I do not anticipate traveling anytime soon."

"Is your illness that serious?" Her brows drew together. "You don't look sick."

"I am not *ill*, per se." The Duchess of Southwick's cheeks took on a warm, pink glow as she linked her hands together across her belly. "Ambrose and I are expecting."

"Expecting what?" Kitty said blankly.

"A *baby*. Right before Christmas, according to the midwife."

Kitty's gaze went to Mara's covered stomach, then her face, then her stomach again. "I'm . . . going to be an aunt?" Logically, she knew that was the typical order of things. A proposal, a wedding, and then a baby. But it was different when it was her sister. Different when it was *her* little niece or nephew growing inside of Mara's belly. "I'm going to be an aunt!"

"The *best* aunt," said Mara, smiling through another onslaught of tears. "This is our chance to do it over. To raise a child who knows only love and kindness."

"You'll be a wonderful mother. You have been for me."

"Oh, Kitty."

Laughing and crying, the two sisters hugged each other tight.

Chapter Fourteen

"Would you care to go for a walk?" After a rainy day filled with both exciting news and much reflection, Kitty had woken the next morning to a clear blue sky and a newfound sense of determination. Because Mara was right. She *did* deserve to love and be loved. Unfortunately, the person she wanted to do both of those things with was currently staring at her as if she'd sprouted a second head overnight.

"A walk?" William repeated, lowering his coffee. He was reading the newspaper in the conservatory, his preferred room to take his breakfast whenever they were at Radcliffe Park. Bright and airy, with a wall of windows that extended all the way up to the domed ceiling paneled in imported teak, it was the most recent addition to the manor, designed by William himself.

Gliding her fingers across the shiny green leaves of a potted orange tree, she wandered up to the table and leaned her hip against it. With the intention of making William's tongue wag, she'd paired her boring black mourning dress with a seafoam shawl and matching tourmaline necklace that dipped low into her cleavage. Her hair was swept off her neck and away from her face in a style she knew he preferred, the blonde curls held in place with pearl studded combs. A subtle streak of kohl along her lash line, a dab of beeswax on her lips, and a spritz of floral perfume on the inside of her wrists had completed her toilette.

"Yes. I thought we might walk through the peach orchards. They should be blooming. We can bring a picnic basket with us."

"A picnic basket?"

Was there an echo in the room?

"A wicker box that is typically filled with different cuts of meats, cheeses, and bread," she provided helpfully. "Usually paired with a blanket to sit upon."

"I am aware of what a picnic basket *is*, Katherine." A muscle ticked in his jaw as he met her gaze with cool, unreadable eyes as dark as his coffee. "What I don't know is why you would have any interest in bringing one on a walk. Or going on a walk to begin with, for that matter."

"I walk," she said defensively, crossing her arms.

"To the shops. From the carriage to the theater. Across a ballroom."

Oh, why did he have to be so bloody *difficult*? Her first instinct was to snap at him. Or to turn on her heel and make a dramatic exit. But after reminding herself why she was there in the first place, she did neither. Mostly because she was determined to find a way to make this marriage work even if it killed her. And a little bit because William was right. She really did detest walking for the sake of walking. But she knew that *he* liked it. Along with riding horses. More than that would be pure speculation. Because the sorry truth was that she really didn't know her husband as much as she should have.

But she was ready to learn.

"Come with me," she implored, touching his arm. "I should like us to spend some time together. If you don't want to go to the orchards, then we can go somewhere else. We can go anywhere you'd like."

His bicep tensed beneath the light grip of her hand. "The peach orchards are fine. I've been meaning to take stock of our inventory since we lost three dozen saplings to blight."

And business, she added silently. Walking, horses, and business.

But there was more to William than that. More than the gruff front he was presenting to her this morning. There was the side of him that had kissed her in the moonlight. The side of him that had given her a lilac bloom. The side of him that had defended her against a monster. The side of him that had refused to give her up, even when giving up would have been easier than holding on.

"Wonderful," she said, striving for a cheerful tone. "I'll gather a few things and meet you in the hall."

⇛⇚

THE PATH TO the peach orchards was winding and slick from the previous day's rain. Twice, Kitty almost fell, and twice, William caught her, holding onto her waist just long enough to ensure she had her balance before taking his arm away.

"You can turn around and go back," he remarked as they approached the crest of a deceptively steep knoll where the first rows of trees began, tucked in between two sloping hills to ensure protection from the wind. "I can assess the saplings on my own."

"Go—go back?" she said, struggling to pull air into her burning lungs. Sweat was pouring down her face and she'd lost all feeling in her toes. Her beautifully constructed curls were hanging in a limp tangle and she was fairly certain she had kohl smeared across her nose. Anyone who found walking, particularly walking through natural terrain, a suitable hobby was clearly deranged. It was torture. Pure, absolute torture. Why, she would have rather been the last person to hear about a new silhouette design being unveiled at Madame Bouchard's than this! "Why—why on earth would I do that? This—this is so very enjoyable!"

She tried to pair her words with a valiant smile as she looked at William over her shoulder. Instead, the smile turned into a pained grimace when her ankle turned and she went sliding sideways with a screech, her arms spinning wildly. He caught her with a curse and this time, he didn't let her go, but rather held her pinned against his chest, his brows a jagged, stormy line above flashing brown eyes.

"Katherine, that's enough. Return to the house before you seriously injure yourself or worse."

"I'm—I'm *fine*," she gasped. "Just . . . just a tad winded. We must be at a different elevation."

"You're wearing slippers." The both looked down to where the toes of her satin dancing shoes were peeking out from beneath the dirt-covered hem of her dress.

She'd worn them—against Emily's advice—because they showed off the trimness of her ankles and the embroidered swirls on the side paired perfectly with her shawl. But she'd dropped her shawl several yards back and the poor slippers were so filthy that the delicate lines of blue thread were nearly impossible to discern.

Kitty lifted her chin. "I'll have you know these are my most comfortable pair of shoes."

"Are they?" William challenged, his mouth forming a superior male smirk. "How many blisters do you have?"

Too many to count.

"It's like walking on a cloud. If you'll release me, I'd like us to continue. Surely we must be almost there."

Please, please let us be almost there.

His smirk fading into a frown, he studied her intently for a moment, his thumbs making absent-minded circles on the curve of her hips as he continued to support her exhausted, blister-riddled feet.

Had she ever noticed the tiny flecks of gold in his irises before, she wondered? Or the blond curl that refused to stay with the rest and instead dropped low over his temple in a rakish wave? Or the line of sun-kissed skin above the fold of his cravat? Surely she had. She'd known this man intimately, in any manner of positions. But perhaps blind passion was just that—blind. And while she knew what William looked like, had she ever stopped to truly appreciate how all of his different parts made up the whole of who he was?

His eyes were from his mother's father, the only person in his family that he'd ever spoken of with any sort of genuine affection and whose portrait hung in his study.

His hair was a touch long because he had a habit of getting too involved with whatever business project he was working on and skipped his weekly sessions with Stevens.

His skin was tanned because he loved being outdoors on the back of a horse, or in an open carriage, or hiking through the Godforsaken wilderness to take inventory of fruit saplings, a job that could have easily been relegated to one of their five gardeners.

"Yes," he said finally, relinquishing his grip on her waist to pick up the picnic basket he'd dropped. "We're almost there."

They resumed walking in measured silence and when the peach orchard was at last within sight—approximately eighty-seven years after they'd started their journey—Kitty wasn't ashamed to say that she shed a tear.

"There," said William, pointing toward the left. "Those trees are the most mature and will give us the best shade. Pick whatever one you like."

The orchard *was* beautiful, Kitty acknowledged grudgingly as she chose one of the older trees whose twisted, gnarled branches had spread out over time to create a natural canopy for their picnic. Peach trees dressed in green and adorned with pale pink flowers stretched out in orderly rows as far as the eye could see. Lush strips of grass dotted with yellow dandelions bisected the rows and bees and butterflies, their wings flapping busily, flew from bloom to bloom, filling the air with a pleasant kind of buzzing. Altogether, the vibrant landscape was a far cry from the dingy, dirty streets of London and the lovely serenity was almost—almost—worth the walk.

A light breeze tickled the loose tendrils at Kitty's nape and helped dry the sheen of perspiration on her forehead as she helped William unfold a large, checkered blanket before sinking gratefully onto the soft fabric in a muddled heap of aching limbs and sore toes.

"Here," he said, taking one look at her and reaching into the basket. "Drink this."

She tried her best not to guzzle the tart lemonade he poured her, but she wasn't completely successful. It felt like liquid gold going down her parched throat and the little moan of pleasure that spilled from her lips was the same sound she made when she came, a tiny detail that did not go unnoticed by William if the sudden flare of heat in his gaze was any indication.

They had not been together since the night he had told her that he'd give her the moon, but not a divorce. His father's passing had kept them both busy in different ways and while she had secretly yearned for William's touch in the quiet night, she hadn't sought it out. Stubbornness was a difficult trait to quell . . . but she was going to do her damned best to try.

"Better?" he asked, crossing his legs out in front of him. The tan breeches he wore clung attractively to his thighs, showcasing rigid lines of muscle courtesy of all his rigorous proclivities. And the sizable bulge between his legs was also worthy of appreciation. But as tempted as she was to run a hand along his leg, Kitty forced herself to still her arm.

Desire, lust, passion . . . those were not the areas where their marriage was falling short. If anything, they were almost *too* good at making love, at giving in to their baser instincts and using their bodies to distract themselves from their real problems.

Trust, honesty, vulnerability . . . *that* was what they needed to work on.

For once, sex would have to be secondary, as disappointing as that was.

"Much," she said, finishing the lemonade and smacking her lips together with an audible *pop*. "Are you hungry?"

"Starved," William said, but he wasn't looking at the picnic basket . . . and the hungry glint in his eyes had her pressing her own thighs together beneath the folds of her skirts.

Perhaps they could talk *after* he ravished her, she reasoned. Surely there wouldn't be any harm in that. Except it would be the same pattern they'd repeated again and again, and wasn't that the definition of lunacy?

"Good." Her stare slipped to his groin and she gritted her teeth. Blast it, this was going to be harder than she'd thought. "I'll—I'll get out the plates."

>>><<<

BEMUSED, WILLIAM WATCHED his wife prepare their picnic meal with all the focus of a French chef. To the best of his knowledge, Kitty had neither cooked nor plated a single piece of food during their marriage. He wasn't even sure if she had a hand in menu preparations. But to look at her now, one would almost be tricked into believing she was creating a culinary masterpiece comprised of slabs of hard cheeses, thinly sliced pieces of smoked ham, and a variety of fruits.

"Do you need any help?" he asked, his head canting to the side as she placed a fig atop a pile of cheese and it promptly rolled off to the side.

"No, I can manage." She waved him off with an irritated flick of her wrist. "Stay over there. *Far* over there."

Eyebrows rising, he did as she asked. Kitty had been acting strangely ever since she'd arrived at Radcliffe Park. Yesterday, after returning from a visit with her sister, she had complimented his tailcoat out of the blue. And today she'd wanted to go on this walk and have a picnic, of all things. An activity he vaguely recalled bringing up when he'd first courted her and one that she'd soundly dismissed.

"*You want me to eat? On the ground? With the ants? Isn't that what they invented tables for?*"

Now here she sat, on a blanket in an orchard, making a meal fit for a king . . . or a marquess. Her slippers kicked off to the side, her hair tossed over her shoulder, her blue eyes—brighter and bolder since she'd accidentally wiped the kohl from her lash line—narrowed in concentration.

Truth be told, he preferred her like this. William knew that Kitty took great pride in her appearance, in her elaborate hair styles and her opulent gowns and her glittering jewelry—all the things she hadn't been able to have before they were married. But while most women used clothes and accessories to enhance their appearance, he was of the opinion that the dresses, the curls, and the necklaces merely competed with Kitty's natural beauty. There wasn't a roll of silk fabric or a diamond on earth that could compare. She was as she had been the first night they met: an enchanting creature without equal.

Which was going to make letting her go that much harder.

"Here you are," she said, all but thrusting a plate at him over the top of the basket.

But instead of reaching for the artistically styled oval of meat and cheese, he grasped her wrist, his long fingers easily encircling the slender, birdlike bones. His thumb sought and found her pulse, its rapid flutter revealing that beneath her wall of composure resided a tempest of lascivious yearning as hot and wild as his own.

The plate fell to the ground, sending grapes rolling across the blanket when he yanked her forward and she tipped onto her knees, her lips forming an *o* of surprise. Then her cheeks heated, those gorgeous blue eyes went dark, and he could have sworn she mumbled "to bloody hell with it" right before she flung herself against him with such power that they both went toppling backward off the blanket and into the grass.

Mine was the only thought that reverberated through his head when he fastened his mouth to hers and drank in lightning. Because that's what Kitty was—lightning in a goddamned bottle. Impossible to contain but glorious to behold.

Tasting her with greedy licks of his tongue, he grasped her hips and centered her over his pulsing manhood, rucking up her skirt and petticoat. She slowly dipped her pelvis, grazing her velvet heat along the swollen length of his staff, and he saw stars as an explosion of lust-filled fire shot straight into his veins. His fingers tangled in her hair, golden ribbons curling around his knuckles when he deepened the kiss, demanding she give him more. Demanding she give him *everything*. If this was to be the last time they made love, he needed the memory of it sustain him for a lifetime. He needed it to brand his fucking soul.

Her nails skimmed across his chest as she snatched his shirt open, then busied themselves with the buttons at the front flap of breeches while her mouth—her hot, heavenly mouth—began a long, wandering descent along the contracted lines of his abdomen.

He sucked in a breath when she traced the outline of his cock with tiny, lapping flicks of her tongue and expelled it on a jagged hiss when she took him between her lips. Lifting himself up on his elbows, he watched with shuttered eyes and clenched fists as her gorgeous head bobbed up and down, taking his generous girth as far into her mouth as she could manage before circling the rounded tip already damp with semen.

All around them, the world continued to move. Soft, fluffy white clouds rolled lazily across a sky of brilliant blue. Birds fluttered from tree to tree while butterflies danced from branch to branch, mesmerized by the nectar contained within the pink flowers that would be round, ripe peaches come late summer. The earth turned. The breeze blew. But here, in the middle of an orchard, time stood still.

It stood still when Kitty cupped below his shaft and gently squeezed while she took him deeper. It stood still when his control threatened to snap and he dragged her up his body to sit on his stomach as a siren would in a pool of seawater, her head thrown back, her mane cascading over her shoulders in a pool of shimmering gold. It stood still when he ripped feverishly at her bodice, tearing delicate lace and tiny pearl buttons. It stood still when she touched her own breasts, pleasuring herself with a low, throaty purr while his vision blurred at the edges.

When he couldn't take it anymore, when the thread of his control had been cut to a single tenuous cord, he took her under him, raising her little feet on either side of his neck as he quenched his thirst with her wet quim. On a cry, she tilted her hips higher, offering her slick folds to him on a table set with green grass and wildflowers.

"William," she gasped, writhing from side to side. "William, I can't take much—"

"You can," he growled, his voice vibrating against her clitoris. "You *will*."

The inside of her thighs trembled when she came, her heels digging into the corded muscle on his back. Before she had begun her descent he pushed her ruthlessly over the edge again, using his hand and tongue in wicked tandem.

Mine, he thought again when her legs quivered and then dropped, limply, to the ground. Shifting onto his haunches, he took himself in hand, stroking rhythmically from base to tip as Kitty lay sprawled before him with her eyes glazed and her lips parted. His breathing quickened when he approached his own release, his cock still wet from her mouth and his own arousal, allowing his palm to move rapidly up and down the marble flesh. Then his breath stopped altogether when her pupils sharpened and she sat up, staying his hand just as he reached the precipice of his own aching desire . . .

<hr />

IT WAS A good thing they were outside, Kitty thought absently as she curled her fingers around William's throbbing cock. Were they in the house, surely the curtains would have gone up in flames by now. The things he'd done to her with his tongue . . . on a delicious shiver, she glided her hand up his chest and then around his neck, pulling herself upward. Grass tickled her knees as they came together for another drugging kiss, the sensation paling in comparison to the lick of fire that shot through her when she arched her hips and took him inside of her.

Inch by decadent inch, Kitty filled herself with William... the power of controlling their passion nearly as intoxicating as the passion itself. A half smile curved her lips when she began to lift herself up and he snarled like a savage dog, his broad hands encompassing her entire waist as he yanked her back down.

She gasped, her thighs clamping around his torso, her nails scratching across his shoulders. They began to move seamlessly together, each instinctively sensing what the other wanted exactly when they wanted it. Beyond the hazy, erotic pleasure of lovemaking they often struggled to have a civil conversation, but under a canvas of endless cerulean, with sunlight dappling their skin and the sweet scent of flowers mingling with the musky perfume of desire, their bodies were poetry in motion.

William splayed his hand across the small of her back and then dipped lower, sliding under her bottom to bring them even closer, his possessive hold undulating with the restless rhythm of her hips. A rhythm that began to increase in tempo as they both soared toward the peak, her mewling whimpers drowned out by his harsh, heavy breaths.

"Come for me *now*," he ordered and for once, Kitty obeyed without question, sobbing out his name into his neck as she convulsed around him, her delicate muscles tightening like an iron sheath around his phallus. He joined her in ecstasy a mere half breath behind, his heartbeat a thunderous roar against her breast as he clutched her to his sweat-slicked body, his chin a heavy weight on her shoulder while a shudder racked through him.

Dazedly, Kitty noted she was still wearing her dress, the bodice torn beyond repair and her drawers ripped through the middle. Shoving her wrinkled skirts below her thighs and her hair out of her eyes, she lay down beside William when he stretched out on the blanket, his clavicle forming the perfect nook for her cheek to nestle into as her index finger made a series of lazy swirls across the broad expanse of his chest while her heightened senses gradually returned to their natural state.

For an indiscernible length of time, there was only the soothing sound of nature. Birds calling. Bees buzzing. Wind whispering through the branches. There was a sense of . . . of fullness in her that she was hard pressed to describe. Of ease. Of calm. Only when she truly put her mind to it did she realize what it was.

Contentment.

Pure, utter contentment.

And then, with six little words, William brought it all crashing down.

CHAPTER FIFTEEN

"KATHERINE, I'LL AGREE to the divorce."

"What?" Caught halfway between drowsiness and dream, Kitty lifted her head, certain she'd misheard. "What did you say?"

He sat up, buttoning his breeches and then reaching for his shirt to cover the red streaks crisscrossing his back courtesy of her nails. "I said that I'll do it. I will agree to the divorce. Why do you look surprised?" he asked, the coldness in his voice all the more slicing given the way he'd just made her burn. "This is what you want. What you've been asking for. What you've been begging for."

"I've never *begged* a day in my life." She stood upright as the haze cleared from her mind and indignation—followed closely by hurt—took its place. Drawing her bodice closed, she scowled up at him as he rose to his feet and pulled on his ebony riding coat. "Where is this coming from?"

"Where is this coming from?" he repeated, his brows soaring. "*You*, Katherine. It's coming from you. How many times have you stormed into my study? How many doors have you slammed on your way out?"

She *did* like to slam doors, Kitty admitted. It was the sound they made as she quit the room. A perfect punctuation mark on a dramatic exit. But that didn't mean—

"I wish for you to be happy, Katherine. That's what *I* want." Fully dressed, he towered over her, every single inch the domineering Marquess of Kentwood while she felt dowdy and disheveled in comparison, a pauper masquerading as a princess. "If this is what it takes, then so be it. You know as well as I that a divorce will be difficult to obtain and likely ruin your reputation, but I'll ensure that you shall want for nothing. You can have Radcliffe Park if you'd like it, along with Hill House in London. The household as well."

Dimly, Kitty registered that she was stepping on a grape. The fruit was squished between her toes. Just as William was squishing her heart beneath his heel. "I don't want Radcliffe Park!" she cried, holding her dress closed with one hand while she flung the other out into the air. "I don't want Hill House. They don't matter. Not really. I want . . . I want . . ."

"Yes?" William said, a peculiar light in his eye as he took a step toward her. "What do you want, Kitty? What do you really want? Because all I want is you. I've made that clear from the beginning."

Her throat worked convulsively. "I want . . ."

"Only when Ambrose was vulnerable with me and I with him, only when we trusted each other with our innermost thoughts and feelings, did our garden start to grow and blossom into the love that we have today."

"I want a weekly allowance. Double what I have now. And a driver at my beck and call."

William's gaze dimmed. His shoulders sagged. "Whatever you'd like."

Was that it, she thought with an irrational surge of anger as he collected their plates and began to fold up the picnic blanket. Was that as hard as he was going to fight her? As he was going to fight for *them*? And damn her pride. *Damn* it. But if he couldn't tell her that he loved her, couldn't he at least fight harder?

He has been, a small voice of reason intruded. *He has been fighting. All along. Perhaps he's tired. Perhaps you both are. Perhaps . . . perhaps there's nothing left to fight* for.

"I don't believe that," she whispered. "I can't."

"Are you coming?" The basket under his arm, William jerked his chin toward the path. "I'll send word to my solicitor this afternoon. It will likely take him several weeks to get everything in order before a petition can be sent."

"No, I am going to walk through the orchards for a while." Somehow it was worse that they weren't fighting. Or yelling. That there were no doors to slam. No angry tears to cry. It made it more permanent somehow. More solemn. And she could have said something. She willed herself to say something. Anything that would stop him. That would make him reconsider. But he was right. This *was* what she'd asked for. Again and again. She *should* have been happy. Ecstatic, even. Instead, she didn't know if she'd ever felt so miserable. Still, she managed a smile as she raised her chin and held onto her stubbornness and her damned pride as if her life depended upon it. "I'll see you for dinner."

"Be careful walking back."

Her smile turned brittle at the edges. "I will be."

⟫⟫⟪⟪

THE SUN WAS nearly setting by the time Kitty returned to the manor. She hadn't meant to stay so long in the orchards, but wandering through the long, flowering rows had given her the clarity—and the courage—that she'd been so desperately lacking when William had caught her off guard with his announcement.

Because it *did* take courage to be vulnerable with the person who had the power to hurt you the most. If she kept her guard up, if she kept part of her heart shielded, then William couldn't destroy all of it. It was a trick she'd learned growing up with a father who could give her a tin necklace one moment and a clip on the jaw the next. But the problem with shielding part of your heart was that that part stayed in the shadows. Without the sun, it never had the opportunity to grow. Without the sun, it could never bloom into something truly beautiful. Eventually, it would wither. Eventually, it would die. And whatever chance she and William might have had of creating a life together would die along with it.

"Stevens." Her husband's valet was the first servant she encountered when she entered the house via a side door, her steps muffled by a thick runner and her hands strategically placed over her chest to disguise the state of her bodice. "Where is my husband?"

The valet stopped short, his beady eyes narrowing to thin slits in the dimly lit hall. "I fail to see how Lord Kentwood's location is of your concern."

He knew, she thought. Somehow, Stevens knew about the divorce. Either William had told him—which she doubted, knowing her husband's penchant for privacy—or the little toad had read the correspondence intended for the solicitor. Regardless, she wasn't about to let him treat her in such a condescending manner. She was still William's wife. And if she had her way, she always would be.

"If you won't tell me, then I'll find him myself." She tried to go past the valet, but he blocked her path and she stopped short, staring at him incredulously. "Move out of the way, Stevens."

"The servants' stairway is behind you," the valet sneered. "Best start getting acquainted with it now, as that's all you'll be using once Lord Kentwood is finally rid of you. It took him long enough, but at last he's come to his senses."

Kitty's jaw dropped. She knew that Stevens had never liked her, but she hadn't known his dislike had extended so far into hate. "You cannot speak to me like that!"

Stevens merely crossed his arms. "When you go, don't forget your disgusting little street urchin. A bitch should leave with all of its fleas."

This time Kitty didn't think, she just reacted. Not in defense of herself, but of Jack. She had grown up with a man's cruel taunts ringing in her ear.

Jack wouldn't.

A slap was a woman's traditional weapon, but she knew from personal experience that a curled fist driven into the kidney hurt worse. Stevens grunted and leaned forward when she punched him. She tried to squeeze past but he stuck out his foot and she tripped, landing hard on her hands and knees, the carpet absorbing the worst of her fall. In a flash, she was a child again. Running from a monster in the dark. Except this time, she wasn't helpless. This time, she had more to fight for than herself.

"Get *off* me!" she shouted when he grabbed her ankle, his fingers digging painfully into bone. She tried to kick but he heaved himself on top of her legs, pinning her to the floor. And when he clamped his hands around her hips an old, familiar greasy sickness rose in her throat.

"He never should have married you," Stevens panted as he crawled his way up her body, using his weight as leverage. She cried out when he slammed his elbow into her back, her arms buckling from the pressure. "You aren't even fit to be his mistress, let alone bear the Colborne name. You're a common guttersnipe that reached too far above her station and now—*aargh!*" The valet's voice cut short on a gargled yelp and Kitty sucked in a wheezing breath when he was thrown sideways into the wall with such force that a painting came crashing down on his head and he slumped, unconscious, to the ground.

"*Katherine.* Are you all right?" William scooped her right up off the floor, holding her cradled against his chest as if she weighed no more than a sack of feather down. Without so much as a glance at the valet who had loyally served him for more than a decade, he carried Kitty straight into his study, closed the door with a kick of his heel, and laid her gently on a sumptuously upholstered sofa that enveloped her in the sweet, earthy scent of leather.

"I am fine." She considered, briefly, playing the damsel in distress. Flinging a hand across her temple, making a few pitiful noises, and hinting that a brand-new piece of jewelry would surely mend whatever ailed her. But taking a situation and twisting it to her advantage was what the old Kitty would have done. And while she didn't consider herself completely reformed, she was *trying* to be better. "Stevens got the worst of it. We should probably send for a doctor."

"Stevens is a dead man," William said with flat, quiet calm.

"He didn't hurt me." To prove her point, she sat up, bringing her knees to her chest. Aside from a dull throbbing between her shoulder blades, she *did* feel shockingly fine. But she didn't want to consider what might have happened had her husband not arrived when he did.

"He put his hands on you." Banked fury flashed in William's gaze. "He *touched* you."

"Then demote him to a footman, or sack him entirely. I don't care." To Kitty's surprise, she truly didn't. Stevens wasn't important. But William was. "I was on my way in from the orchards. I was looking for you."

William sat heavily in a chair opposite the sofa and scrubbed a hand down his face. "If you want to know if I've written off to the solicitor—"

"No, I don't. Well, yes I do," she corrected with an errant turn of her wrist. "Because you'll need to call the letter back. Or send another on its heels. Whatever is most efficient."

"What should this second letter say?" he asked, his countenance unreadable.

"That there will be no divorce." Kitty took a deep breath. "Ever."

A light flickered in William's gaze, then was quickly extinguished as he sagged back in the chair and stared past her at the wall, a muscle ticking in his jaw. "You needn't play any more games, Katherine. I'm giving you what you want."

"What I want ... what I *really* want ..." When her voice quavered, she borrowed one of Jack's more creative favorite curses before plowing determinedly ahead. "It's you, William. It's been you since the first night we met and it will continue to be you until I draw my last breath. I don't want a divorce. I don't want to run. I want to stay right here, with you. Well, not always right *here*," she amended. "I should like to return to London for the Season when I can wear color again. Black really is the worst shade for my complexion, and—"

"Kitty?"

"Hmm?"

"Be quiet." In one fluid motion, he was off the chair, she was standing wrapped in his arms, and their mouths were together in a kiss that she would have happily let lead to more had he not abruptly stopped and put his hands on her shoulders, forcing distance between them. "I can't . . . I don't know if . . ."

She spread her hands open on his chest, feeling the beat of his heart as her own ached at the pain she saw in his eyes. "It wasn't your fault, William. What happened to Alessandra and my father, it wasn't your fault. Their deaths are not your burden to bear. I should have told you that a long time ago."

A shudder went through him. "I don't deserve—"

"You do," she interrupted. "You do deserve to be loved, William. You do deserve *to* love. You only have to give yourself permission. And if you cannot speak the words aloud, I don't need to have them. Words are just words. You've shown me your love in any manner of ways. I simply didn't want to see it."

He cupped her chin, his thumb stroking her cheek. "You need the words, Katherine," he said huskily. "Every intelligent, strong, and beautiful woman should hear how loved she is. How treasured she is. How valued she is. I fell in love with you that night in the moonlight, and I have loved you every day, every hour, every second since. I love you so much that I was ready to let you go, even though it would have destroyed me. I love you, Lady Katherine Colborne, Marchioness of Kentwood. I should have said it sooner."

"It was worth the wait." Smiling through a sheen of joyful tears, Kitty rose up on her toes and kissed her husband.

Epilogue

Several Months Later

"KITTY! KITTY, COME 'ere, it's *snowing!*" Jack's voice rang through the garland-draped halls of Hill House, causing both Kitty and William to freeze.

"Not a word," Kitty warned in a low voice, wagging her finger in front of her husband's face. They were both occupying the same chair. William was sitting on it and she was sitting on *him*, her skirts rucked up past her knees while his hands clasped her bottom.

After hosting his mother for the past month and her sister for the month before that, this was the first moment of alone time they'd been able to steal during the middle of the day. She wasn't about to let Jack ruin it.

"KITTY! WHERE ARE YE?"

William chuckled softly. "You know she's been hoping for a white Christmas. We can pick this up after dinner."

"It's snow," Kitty groaned even as she slid off to the side and made herself presentable. "Cold, wet, lumpy snow. How exciting can it be?"

"Katherine—"

"I'm going, I'm *going.*" Tromping out of the library and into the parlor where Jack stood with her nose pressed to the window,

Kitty rolled her eyes before she walked up to the sill and peered out at the street beyond where white flecks lightly fell from a gray, overcast winter sky. "You're right. It's snowing. How nice. Did you have a chance to try on the dresses that were delivered from the modiste yesterday? My seamstress will be here in the morning if there are any hems that need to be let down. I swear, you've grown another two inches overnight."

A summer and autumn spent in the country had made Jack sprout like a weed. Her limbs were ganglier than ever and the top of her head nearly reached Kitty's shoulder. Another year, and she'd likely be on her way to catching up to William. She had grown in other ways, too. When she wasn't excited and took the time to work on her pronunciation, her speech was coming along beautifully courtesy of weekly tutoring sessions with a *very* patient instructor. She'd also started dancing lessons and was learning how to properly conduct herself in a public setting. ("Remember your three *s*'s," Kitty reminded her every time they set foot out the door. "No spitting, no shoving, no stealing.") Her hair was still wild, and she wore trousers whenever she could get away with it, but she was gradually showing signs of improvement. And most importantly, she was now officially Kitty and William's ward. The three of them were a family, albeit an unlikely one: the marquess, the wastrel's daughter, and the street urchin. It wasn't exactly the premise of a traditional happily-ever-after but it was *their* happily-ever-after, and that was all that mattered.

Kitty and William still fought. They were both too stubborn not to. But they took care to work through their grievances every single evening before they went to bed, and they never awoke with anger or blame in their hearts.

It wasn't always easy. Then again, perhaps some love—perhaps the most meaningful love—wasn't supposed to be.

"Want to go outside?" Jack asked brightly, ignoring Kitty's question. "I want to make a snowman!"

"There isn't enough snow for a . . ." Kitty sighed as Jack dashed off with a whoop, ". . . snowman."

"Sounds like someone is afraid *their* snowman won't pass muster," William commented from the doorway, his eyes twinkling. He was already dressed for the elements in a scarf and greatcoat. Out of the corner of her eye, she saw Jack running gleefully across the front yard, her head thrown back to catch snowflakes on her tongue.

"There's hardly an inch of snow on the ground," she protested as she let William pull her toward the foyer. He pulled a heavy wool cloak over her shoulders and pinched her bottom before following her outside, then stood with his arm tucked snug around her waist while they watched their daughter play.

"Aren't ye going to join me?" Jack called out, flinging a shower of white into the air.

"No," said Kitty, already shaking her head. "I don't think so. Emily just curled my hair, and—*William!*" Her mouth opened in shock when her husband—her loving, caring, doting husband—dropped a snowball down her back. "Oh, now you've done it!"

Jack clapped her approval as the Marquess and Marchioness of Kentwood scrambled into fighting positions, both of them scooping up as much snow as they could find.

"Ready, set, FIRE!" Kitty yelled, launching a ball through the air before quickly ducking behind a tree. She heard a snowball splat against the bark and grinned triumphantly, then squealed when she was pummeled from behind. "Jack! Whose side are you on?"

"A thief is always on her own side," Jack said with a smirk.

Kitty and William exchanged a glance.

"On the count of three?" she asked, arching a brow.

"What are ye doing?" Jack said warily.

"One," William nodded, molding another snowball.

"Why are ye looking at me like that?"

"Two."

"Stop counting."

"THREE!" they shouted in unison before they launched a coordinated attack that ended with all of them breathless from laughing and covered in snow from head to toe.

"Go and get a bath, then come down to the parlor for hot chocolate," Kitty instructed Jack, giving her a nudge toward the stairs. She waited until Jack had scampered off before turning toward her husband. "You shouldn't have done that, you know."

"Done what?" he said, all roguish innocence.

"Hit me with a snowball! I'm your wife. And now I'm freezing," she complained with an exaggerated shiver.

"Well in that case," said William, drawing her into his arms and nuzzling her neck. "Let me warm you up . . ."

※※※

IN A SLIGHTLY larger house a few streets away, another couple was warming themselves in front of a roaring fire while snow continued to fall from a darkening sky.

"I believe I'll go to bed early tonight," Mara said, muffling a yawn. "I cannot seem to keep my eyes open."

"Is it the baby?" Ambrose pressed a protective hand to her swollen belly as his dark brows knitted with concern. "Have contractions started? Should I fetch Dr. Chadwick?"

"No," Mara said for what had to be the hundredth time. Smiling affectionately, she linked her fingers with her husband's over their growing babe and her heart swelled when she felt an answering flutter . . . followed by a less comfortable jab to her bladder. "I am not having contractions, and Dr. Chadwick has assured me that they won't start before Christmas Eve. I'm just tired, Ambrose. Which she has assured me is completely normal at this stage of my pregnancy."

"How can she be sure? We should get a second opinion. Yes, that's what we'll do. First thing in the morning—"

"First thing in the morning, I will still be asleep. It'll be all right," she said gently. "The babe will arrive when he or she is ready. I don't want a second opinion. We came to London specifically to be close to Dr. Chadwick, as you know that she refuses to travel. And Dr. Chadwick is going to be the one who delivers our baby."

"I'm just worried. For both of you," Ambrose murmured, lowering his head to press a kiss to the top of her stomach. "If anything goes wrong—"

"Everything will go splendidly. So long as I get myself off to bed."

"Let me help you up the stairs."

"I can still climb steps, Ambrose," said Mara with an exasperated laugh. She knew that her husband meant well. She also knew that he was accustomed to being in control and his anxiousness stemmed from not having any in this particular situation. "Stay down here. Have a glass of brandy. I'll call you if I need you." She paused. "I *will* need help getting out of this sofa."

It took a few heaves, but once she was finally free she bid Ambrose goodnight and waddled into the foyer. She was just about to start her arduous journey up the stairs when a pounding on the door stopped her. Before the butler could intervene, the door swung inward and Dr. Abigail Chadwick, covered in a dusting of snow, stumbled inside.

The American doctor was a rather peculiar woman. But behind her crooked gold spectacles and big green eyes was an unprecedented level of genius. She wasn't just a physician. She was the *best* physician in England, her talents often ignored or unnoticed due to her gender.

"Dr. Chadwick?" Mara said in bemusement. "Did we have an appointment I forgot about? Oh my. Did Ambrose send for you? Because I told him—"

"I require your assistance," Abigail interrupted. "You have to hide me."

"Hide you?" she said, startled. "Hide you from what?"

"Not what, *whom*." The doctor's eyes darted nervously behind her spectacles as she looked over her shoulder, as if preparing to be set upon at any second. "My husband. The Earl of Lancaster. He's here."

About the Author

Jillian Eaton grew up in Maine and now lives in Pennsylvania on a farmette with her husband and their three boys. They share the farm with a cattle dog, an old draft mule, a thoroughbred, and a mini-donkey—all rescues. When she isn't writing, Jillian enjoys spending time with her animals, gardening, reading, and going on long walks with her family.

www.ingramcontent.com/pod-product-compliance
Ingram Content Group UK Ltd.
Pitfield, Milton Keynes, MK11 3LW, UK
UKHW021005030225
454602UK00012B/593

9 781965 539811